As a young man, the author was engaged on the MCC ground staff at Lord's Cricket Ground and played several matches at the famous Mecca of cricket prior to his National Service in the Royal Air Force. On returning to civvy street, he worked at numerous jobs: cricket coach, groundsman, insurance salesman. It was then that he began writing and went on to self-publish some of his novels.

Dedication

To all my family and friends

.

John Costello

SATURDAY NIGHT HEROES

AUSTIN MACAULEY PUBLISHERS™

LONDON · CAMBRIDGE · NEW YORK · SHARJAH

A CIP catalogue record for this title is available from the British Library.

ISBN 9781788239769 (Paperback)
ISBN 9781788239776 (Hardback)
ISBN 9781788239783 (E-Book)

www.austinmacauley.com

First Published (2018)
Austin Macauley Publishers Ltd™
25 Canada Square
Canary Wharf
London
E14 5LQ

Chapter 1

Once again, it's Monday morning, and I'm sitting at my office desk waiting for her to come through the door. I say the desk is mine, but in actual fact, and as everyone else is well aware, it's nothing of the sort really. Just a figure of speech. The desk belongs, as does everything else in this office, to Mr Tarp of Tarp's Bathroom & Toilet Accessories, the firm I work for. I'm employed here as a clerk cum office boy cum bloody tea maker, and I'm flaming well-browned off with it. Browned off with the dull, droll job. I need a change, I know that. And not only with my job, but with my whole rotten image. But where is she anyway? She should be here by now. It's the only thing I look forward to each day – her arrival. Carol Shelley's her name. Same age as me – 'bout 18. Her first job, too. Only difference is that I think she enjoys working for old Tarp; she's his secretary.

Not that she started out in this position, mind. Switchboard operator before that. Early promotion because of efficiency and interest shown towards the job and clients is what Tarp put it down to when upgrading her six months after her arrival at the office. Not that Carol can't tackle the job. She can – is very good at it in fact. Just makes me envious, that's all. Envious of that old sod having her to himself from nine till five each working day of the week. A fleeting glance is all I manage to get of her these days. Not like when she worked the switchboard. Plenty of times then when we could talk and pass the time of day. We're not a very big office, see, and apart from Tarp, Carol and myself, there's only dear old Miss Pruce, who – now, incidentally – operates the switchboard in place of Carol, and Mr Jenkins, the wages clerk, works here. There's other staff working over in the yard where the various bathroom and toilet items are stored, old Jock Wilson being in charge of them as yard foreman. But we don't see much of them really. Now and again, one of us – usually me – has to pop over to check on some item or other to see if it's in stock. Other than that, we employees of Tarp's only get together when the firm has its annual coach trip outing down to Southend for the day. Had one of these recently, we did, but more about that later.

At the moment, I'm still waiting patiently for Carol to make an appearance on this bright Monday morning of my life. She'll come bouncing through in a minute full of the joys of life, greet me with her usual smile, then disappear to old Tarp's office for the best part of the day. I mean, there was a time once when Carol and I would take lunch together. Admittedly, it was only just 'round the corner at British Rail's cafeteria of our town's main station, but you can get a proper three-course cheap there – soup, dinner, pudding. Only trouble is that the tables rattle when the fast trains come through. Bit sodding noisy as well, I can tell you. Good fun though, especially with old Rosy, the waitress there. P'roxide blonde, blue-eyed, buxom, with the biggest pair of boobs I've ever seen in me life. She's married with three kids to her name as well. Some of the jokes she comes out with is nobody's business.

"Wot's yer fancy today then, me luv'lies?" she'd holler, pumping steaming hot water into a huge urn behind the counter, a tray full of empty cups lined up in front of her waiting to be topped up with what some reckoned as the best cuppa in town.

We would catch her eye. "Peaches an' cream, please, Rosy!"

"Two peaches for the luv-birds, 'Arry!" Rosy would shout above the din to Harry, the cook, who's out of sight in the kitchen. Don't do a bad meal neither. Quiet bloke, Harry. Hardly ever speaks. When he does, you'd need a hearing aid to make out what he's saying.

"Eh! 'ear the one about the Irishman what couldn't get up in the morning?" Rosy would crack a joke. Pretty good some of them, too.

It's a fairly busy cafeteria, catering for the true working classes. Always packed out with geezers popping in and out all day for a cuppa, railway workers, postmen. All of us uses it, and nearly all the blokes try making it with Rosy. She won't hear any of it though. Good for a laugh, but strictly, no hanky-panky's with her, mate, I can tell you.

Then out of the blue one day over our peaches, Carol informs me that she's not going to use the place anymore. Was just after her promotion at the office, I remember.

"What's up, getting too posh for us now, are we?" I cracks hurtfully, looking ahead of me over the haze of cigarette smoke that's forever present in this eating house of British Rail and at Rosy as she playfully slaps the hand of old Percy, the electric meter reader, who's trying his hardest to fondle her you know wot's it's.

"Know me better than that, Henry," Carol replies, lighting a fag up to add to the pollution.

Henry's me name, see. Henry Higgins, as it happens. Right bloody name an'all. What some mothers must be thinking when they christen their own kith and kin with handles like that, I just dunno. I ask you – what blokes is famous with them sorta names? No chance, have I?

"And why aren't you coming here any longer, Carol?" My voice betrays the angriness I'm feeling at this particular moment. Choked at the thought of not having our little lunch get-togethers, ain't I?

"Cos Mr Tarp's asked me to have lunch with him in future, that's why."

Carol draws on her cigarette, inhales, blows smoke out hurriedly, averting my gaze in the process.

"Cocky bitch!" I thinks to meself.

"Has he now?" I then says, all highfalutin', like, wagging me head from side to side. "'Hain't we just coming up in the world then?"

"Don't see any harm in it." She's tapping her cigarette on the side of the ashtray. "Nicer than here any day."

"What is?"

Carol starts to explain, but the 12-45 to Euston suddenly comes hurtling through on Platform 9, drowning her speech.

"Would you mind repeating that?" I asks, after the bleeding commotion and vibrating tables has subsided.

"He's asked me to go with him to his Club for lunch."

"What blasted club?"

She stubs her cigarette out in the messy ashtray, then looks me hard in the eye. "The Conservative Club – where else?"

I stares at her for a moment. "You can't be serious, Carol?" I asks in disbelief.

"Cos I'm serious," she's quick to retaliate, hurriedly gulping the remains of her tea, spilling some on her white blouse. "Nothing wrong in that, is there?"

I leans back in me chair, stuffing me hands in me trouser pockets. "Not much, gal. Bleeding Con-Club. I ask you? Not a bloody Tory, are you?"

"How do you know what I am, Henry?" Her bottom lip is twitching.

"I knows what your old man is then, and it ain't a bleeding conservative neither," I pauses for a moment. "Likes of you and me, gal... Well, we ain't like Tarp and his kind. We're Labour, ain't we? Socialists!"

She's on the defence now. "So doesn't mean I can't use the Club, does it?"

I start to stammer. "N-no, I s'pose not." I'm feeling betrayed. And just as I thought our relationship together was beginning to mean something. "But what about *us*, Carol?"

She touches my hand across the table. "Look, Henry."

"Two sossidge-egg an' chips, please, 'Arry!" Rosy's coarse cry echoes 'round the cafeteria, her hot water machine hissing as she makes a fresh pot of tea.

"I'm looking," I says to Carol, waiting for an explanation after this rude interruption. Bleeding brush off is what she's giving me, I knows it.

"I wanna get on, Henry."

"Watcha mean?"

"Well, now that I am Mr Tarp's personal secretary."

"I knew it – you are getting too big for your boots," I interrupts. She removes her hand.

"Know your trouble, don't you, Henry?" Another interruption follows.

"The train now arriving on platform 7 is the twelve fifty-five to Aylesbury – stopping at..."

"You've got no go in you," Carol lectures me. "You're quite content to let things go on as they are. I mean, don't you ever wanna improve yourself?"

"Watcha mean?"

"Watcha mean – watcha mean, is that the only sentence you're capable of uttering?" She's getting her back up now all right. "Do you wanna stay checking lavatory pans for the rest of your life?"

"Watcha mean?" It's a dumb answer, I know it.

So Carol suddenly stands up and storms off out the place, don't she? Leaves me sitting there like a right bloody lemon. But I'm not running after her. Sod her; if that's the way she wants it. Besides, I ain't finished me pudding yet, have I?

I was annoyed, I can tell you. After all, me and Carol's been close for a long while now. Ever since school days, as it happens. We both live up on the same estate. Her old man works on the railways, same as mine. And here she is about to start going with Mr bloody Tarp to the Con-Club for her lunch in the future. Our type backgrounds, and she- wants to go poncing down the bleeding Tory Club. Not on, is it? Least, I don't think so anyway. She wouldn't be at home with the riff- raff that gets in there, I know. Why the hell she can't stick with her own kind beats me. Ever since that bloody Tarp she's begun changing, Carol. Pity, cos we get on so well together as a rule.

As I say, ever since school days, both of us received second mod education. First spotted her playing netball for the school team. What a pair of legs! One of her mates introduces us, and hey presto! It's love at first sight. Shortly after, it's round her place to meet her folks. Nice couple, friendly. As I say, her old man works for British Rail, same as mine – so we immediately gets on like a train on fire, don't we? In fact Sid – that's her father's name – uses the same Club as me dad at weekends. Labour Club, you know. Carol and I go along sometimes. Have some good nights there, we do. The Club's just round the corner from here – back of Tarp's place, matter of fact. As I say, it's okay there. Gets a bit rowdy some nights with fights breaking out. Not much fun then. But on the whole it's pretty well behaved. Besides, the law's only just up the road if they're needed anytime.

So you can imagine what kind of backgrounds we all come from, can't you? Not that I'm complaining. I'm not – there's far worse off I reckon. That's what makes me mad with Carol and her bleeding getting on bit in life. So – we all wants to get on, don't we? But it's not everyone that gets on, is it? After all, if all us working class was to make it to the top there wouldn't be any of us left to carry out the good work, would there now? That's my philosophy anyway, and it's pretty sensible if you ask me. Stands to reason, don't it? Someone's got to do the work. Think that's half the trouble meself. I mean, there's some people so hell bent with getting on in this world that they forget where they came from originally, and deserts their own kind in the end. Traitors really, ain't they? Don't get me wrong. 'Cos I wants to get on – improve meself, like Carol says. Been giving it some serious thought lately as well. Like I mentioned, I does a bit of singing at weekends in the Labour Club. Or maybe I didn't mention it before? Well, anyway that's what I do sometimes. So perhaps I'll have a go at the pop world – you know – become a pop singer? I've been told that I have a good voice. They all seem to like my stage act. Who knows – I might do just that. I'll have to change me name though. I mean, Henry Higgins! Never make it with a handle like that, will I? Shake Carol, that would. Especially if I made the big time? It was only last month that I bought meself a guitar. Wanna hear it – it's really great! That's what I say about changing me image. Carol's right. Must get meself out of Tarp's place. Dead end there all right. I'd miss Carol though. Not that she'll have much time for me now that she's hobnobbing with this geezer, will she?

"Where's our Carol, Henry?" Rosy enquires, her tea pouring temporarily at an end with the lunchtime rush dying down.

"She's gone," I inform her sadly, noticing that me and old Percy are the only customers left in the place now. Cigarette smoke still lingers above our heads as Rosy lights one up for herself before preparing to wash the dirty dishes.

"You two been fighting, have you?"

I pushes me empty dish across the table. "We had a few words, yeah," I mumble miserably. Used to having Carol sitting opposite, ain't I?

Rosy shoots me a concerned look. "Nothing serious I hope, young'un?"

Old Percy slides his chair back to the wall and gets to his feet. "Be seeing you then, Rosy, gal!" he bids the love of his life farewell.

"Ta – ta, Percy, darlin'. Careful how you go now."

I make a move to leave as well.

"Not to worry, 'Enry, things'll sort themselves out, you'll see. 'Sides, it's nice makin' up, ain't it?"

I gets to the door just as a train races through on Platform 9. "So long, Rosy," I says above the din. I'm not sure whether she hears me or not and I have this strange feeling like I'm not going to be using the place anymore. I mean, if Carol can go off with old Tarp to his bleeding Club, then I can do likewise, I'm sure. Find somewhere different. Someplace other than this bloody railway cafe with its dirty red brick walls. Funny how you can use a place for a long time and not really notice what it looks like from the outside until now, ain't it? Same as the railway station itself. This hasn't changed at all since it was built, I don't think. Me dad has a photo of the place on a wall at home and it looks just the same now as when the flaming picture was taken. Which was ages ago, I know. It's even got the cobblestones out front where the taxis wait and where the Green Line coaches now swing round on their outward journeys. Matter of fact they've only just recently built a bleeding car park at the back of the station after all these years. I ask you? Was in the local paper – it's grand opening. Mayor and his bleeding lot had a special ceremony for it. Champagne and everything. Know what they did? You'll never believe it. They all sat down at a table in the middle of the roadway under the bridge where the new driveway leads up to it sipping glasses of bubbly. Yeh – no joking. 'History in the Making' read the headlines. I ask you? Still, least the old mayor's a labour man, ain't he? Yeah, he's a socialist all right. Got the interest of the community at heart. Had a lot to do with the recent modernisation of our houses up on the estate, he did. Knocked us about a bit – the builders. But it was well worth it in the end. Got central heating now. About time an'all, considering the bleeding estate was built just after the war. Only bit of work they've ever had done to them. Same as the old

Labour Club which lies directly behind the railway station. Badly in need of a face lift this building is. Looks like Fagin's workhouse at the moment with its murky walls, dirty windows and tall, dark chimney pots that reach up to the sky.

Still, s'pose it's a place where the workers can meet over a pint of beer and a chat, like. The mayor himself pops in now and again for a drink. Sat with me mum and dad one Saturday night, he did, watching me perform one of me numbers.

"Orta go on stage, lad," he suggests to me in his broad Yorkshire lingo after I've finished me act.

"Our 'Enry's always liked singin'," me mum, sipping her milk stout, informs him proudly.

"Takes after the old man, don't he?" me dad boasts, lighting himself a cigarette. "Used to call me the singin' railwayman in my younger days you know."

"Get away with you," me mum sniggers.

"Any road – I think you could make a go of it, young Henry, lad," mister mayor adds, sipping his brandy.

So I suppose that's where the idea first comes from with regards to me entering the pop world, like. Question is – how to go about it?

"Why not write away to the BBC," me dad advises after I've tackled him on the subject one morning.

"Do you think he should, Charlie?" me mum, frying breakfast out in the kitchen, queries this piece of advice.

"Don't see why not. Bloody noise some of them makes – he can't do worse, I know."

"Mean travelling up to London?"

"So? Won't cost him, will it? Courtesy of British Rail, if I have anything to do with it. Say – hurry up with those bacon an' eggs, gal – me train's due out in twenty minutes."

"All right, all right – keep your hair on. Doing me best."

Me dad's been picking the day's winners from the Mirror's racing column while this chat is going on. Likes his flutter, the old man. He don't do too bad sometimes.

Then Mum comes through with our breakfasts. "Better shove some coal on that fire before I forget," she says in annoyance with our new fangled heating system.

"I'll do it –I'll do it," me dad comes to her rescue with impatience, getting to his feet and heading in the direction of the coal.

"Why they couldn't leave the fires open… as they were, I'll never know. Blow us all up one day – you see if they don't."

Me mum don't like any sorta change, you see. Not even for the best at times, it would seem.

So you can see what kind of conversation takes place under our roof, can't you. But I seem to be getting away from things. To get back to what I was saying about Carol walking out on me that day in the cafeteria. This all happened last Friday, see. And here am I this Monday morning still waiting for her to make an appearance in the office, like. I haven't seen her at all over the weekend, missing our usual get together this Saturday. Usually pop round to her place then. Her old man and meself might then take ourselves along to the football. My dad sometimes goes with us – if he's not working, that is. Our Club's only fourth division, play quite good football though. Smallish ground, with an average attendance of around four to five thousand each week. Our town's hospital overlooks the pitch. That's another building that could do with a bit of brushing up as well in my opinion. I mean, it's dirty and shabby in appearance for a hospital.

They've recently added a new maternity unit to it; but I'm hardly likely to be using that place, am I? Mind, those proud fathers would be happy if they're football followers, wouldn't they? Cos you can actually watch the game from the windows up there on the top floor. Apart from this facility though it's the same now as it was way back in Florence Nightingale's time, ain't it?

Talking of football, brings me on to a particular sad subject concerning one of me former mates, Eddie, don't it? Bit of a tear away, he was. Unfortunately, he's no longer with us, having lost his life tragically after overdosing on drugs whilst in custody in a remand home. He's in there for stealing cars and of causing actual bodily harm to an opposition football fan, ain't he? Football hooligan, the authorities branded him with. Eddie had always sworn his innocence though. I believed him as well, cos I was there when it was supposed to have happened, weren't I? We had both travelled up to London to watch our Club play an away game one eventful Saturday afternoon last season. A fight broke out when some of the opposition supporters invaded our terraces. The police were called. They waded in, pulling bodies out of the fracas to discover a youngster badly kicked and beaten lying on the ground. Manhandling a dozen of those involved in the incident, the police then marched them away to a waiting van outside the ground to literally bundle them inside and drive off to a police station. Unfortunately, Eddie was among them. Despite my pleas with the cops of his innocence in the matter, they were in no mood to listen. In fact I heard one of them remark angrily: "Ruin our bloody afternoon, will you – we'll soon sort you bastards out, see if we don't!" I'm telling them that Eddie's been with me all the time they were fighting, ain't I? But it's my word against theirs, ain't it? That's how it comes out in the trial as well, despite having our local MP as defence barrister. The mayor pulled a few strings in persuading him to represent Eddie, see. Labour man as well, ain't he?

"You're not bullshitting me on this now, are you, Eddie? You definitely weren't involved in this fight, were you?" he asks his client before taking on the case.

"I swear to God, guvna, I had nuffin to do with it," Eddie assures the geezer, don't he. But it don't do no good and Eddie is found guilty of GBH. We're all devastated, specially his folks. And what with his previous record not helping matters any, he is sent to this bloody remand home, ain't he. Now Eddie's always had a short fuse where authority is concerned, and we learns when visiting him on occasions that the bastards there have been giving him injections to calm down his outbursts when he gets out of hand, ain't they, the shits! Yeah, they keeps pumping him full of this crap, don't they? Eventually he's released; but by this time he's hooked, ain't he? In the home he'd been mixing with other users, like. Consequently, this encourages him to experiment with harder substances which ultimately lead to his untimely death by OD-ing one Saturday night in the ablutions. It's a terrible shock to us all. I still haven't come to terms with it. Heaven knows how his parents are coping. Admittedly, Eddie was no angel and was way out of order in a lot of things he'd done; but no one really believed he deserved this. It left me feeling very angry, especially toward those lying bastard policemen at his so called trial. God! There's something wrong somewhere when an innocent bystander can be fitted up like Eddie was, ain't there? It was nice of that MP to fight in poor Eddie's corner though, weren't it? Not many geezers in his position would take on such a case, I know. But even he had to admit defeat in the end. Makes you wonder if Eddie would still be around if things had gone his way, don't it?

Anyway, life goes on, and while me and Carol's old man is watching the football, my mum and Carol and her mum take themselves off to the bingo, don't they? They enjoy that. Never known them to win anything, mind. Then after tea in the evening we sometimes takes a trip down to the Labour Club for a drink and a sing-song, with me doing me little bit up on stage with me guitar, like. There's other turns as well. Not bad, some of them either. Like old Randy, the singing cowboy. Comes on all dressed up for the part, ten gallon hat, guns and holsters, whip, everything. Sings a good song. Nice voice. No youngster, Randy. He's living with this gorgeous looking gal who likes watching him perform at the Club. Name's Edna, from up north somewhere. Only twenty years of age. Marvellous figure. Should see it. Likes when her Randy sings High Noon.

Me and Carol might fancy going along to the pictures instead though. All depends. Anyhow, we're all one big happy family, ain't we? That is, till Carol gets this idea in her head of going over to the other side, so to speak. I think she means it, too. I mean, she's not in anytime I call round her place over the weekend. Probably hobnobbing it with bleeding Tarp at his Club if the truth is known. Not the same there though, is it? I mean, they don't have entertainment like we do. It's just drink and chat or playing cards and dominoes. They might have an occasional dance. Very rare though. I peeked through the window one day when I was returning to Tarp's office after lunch. They got snooker tables in the back room. But then, so have we at the Labour. I like playing snooker; challenge me old man to a game sometimes. He's a good player. Nearly always beats me though. Matter of fact he's won some cups for being the Club's champion for a number of years when he was younger. Bet Tarp can't boast of that? Bet he's got no bleeding cups?

And by this time the geezer's made his appearance in the office, ain't he? "Good morning, Higgins!" he addresses me, before disappearing behind his door.

I don't answer him, wondering to meself where the hell Carol is.

She's bleeding late, that's for sure. I mean, everyone else is here. Miss Pruce is seated by her switchboard waiting patiently for any calls, and at the same time reading her favourite Mills & Boon romance. Old man Jenkins is busy scratching away in the ledger with his pen working out everyone's wages for the coming week. Not that they will amount to much anyway. Tarp's a stingy sod where money is concerned. And all the while I'm thinking to meself that the place needs a bleeding bomb under it to liven it up, like.

Tarp's office door opens and he's standing there looking all very important and trying to catch me eye. But I won't give way to his bloody superiority, will I? I just sits there pretending I'm checking stock from a sheet of paper in front of me.

"I want you to run over the yard later, Higgins," he informs me. He's a tall geezer, with greying hair and a thin moustache stuck over his lip. What on earth Carol sees in the guy I just don't know. I s'pose he ain't bad looking in some sort of beat up way; but surely she's got no designs on him? I mean, the guy's twice her age, ain't he? Still, he's got security – what most gals want really. "Mayor's wife's ordered a complete new bathroom unit for their house."

"Is that so?" I murmur uninterestedly. Gonna set the old boy back a few quid, I know?

"Check to see if the WD2 models are still in stock, will you? She's got her heart set on this particular one."

Before going back into his office again, and mainly for my benefit, he says in a sarcastic, one-upmanship sort of way: "By the way, Higgins – Miss Shelly won't be in today, in case you are wondering where she is? She wasn't feeling too well last night, so I told her to take the day off."

Ello, 'ello, I thinks to meself. What's our Carol been up to then? All bleeding right, ain't it? Bet he wouldn't give me a day off. Deep down though I'm bloody mad, I can tell you. Seems the geezer has stepped right into my shoes, don't it? Huh! Well I'll show him then. Carol, too. I'll bloody well show them just what our Henry can do.

So I takes meself off over the yard to check on the mayor's bathroom unit don't I? And all the while I'm thinking about this pop star thing, determined more than ever now to go ahead with me plans in this direction, like. I'll make it big, that's what I'll do. Just wait and see if I don't. No more checking lavatory pans for our Henry here. Sod it! I'll take me dad's advice and write away to the BBC.

Chapter 2

So… do you know what happens? The old mayor himself fixes me up with an audition at the BBC, don't he? Seems he's got a friend that works there or something, and he pulls it for me, like. So it's all set up. Handy having someone taking an interest in your well-being, ain't it? You may be wondering why the mayor of our town should be showing this interest. Well… I think it's because of me old man working on the railways. See, the mayor himself used to as well when he was younger – work on the railways, I mean, as a surveyor. Anyway, he informs me and the family of this good news this Saturday night down at the Labour Club.

"I've arranged it all with the BBC for you. Henry," he tells me just after I've performed one of me numbers on stage. "This coming Friday, lad – in London. Make sure you go along now. Chance of a life time for you, Henry."

I sits there sipping me brown ale, me guitar between me knees, not knowing what to say really; but me folks makes up for me lack of words, don't they?

"Our Henry with the BBC? Whatever next?" me mum utters excitedly, attacking her Guinness.

"I keep telling you – it's in the family, ain't it?" me old man boasts proudly.

"Could get yourself lost in London," me mum adds with concern. "Never know who you're likely to meet up there?"

She's a dear old soul, and is generally worried about me welfare, ain't she? It's not as if I've never been to London before, is it? Me and Carol goes sometimes to see a movie or maybe to have a drink in the West End somewhere. Makes a change, don't it?

"What time's he gotta be there, Will?" me dad asks. Old man's on Christian name terms with the mayor, ain't he? Nothing like sticking together, is there? Old Will has a go at his brandy. "Ten thirty in the mornin', Charlie," he replies in the same intimate fashion.

"Lad should be all right for a train… I'm on early runs to Euston that week."

I nods me head in appreciation of this fact. Certainly saves me a few bob, don't it?

The mayor hands me a piece of paper. "That's the audition address you've to go to, lad," he informs me, lighting a cigar.

At this point of the conversation the Club's compere jumps up on stage to hug the microphone. "And now, ladies an' gentlemen! We have our regular singing country an' western singer to offer us some real first class entertainment! So a big 'and if you please…! Here he is – our very own – Randy Bates!"

The old piano in the corner comes to life along with the set of drums as a couple of musicians bring them to life to accompany Randy who's coming on stage cracking his whip and firing his six shooter and yodelling his way through Ghost Riders in the Sky.

"Yippee – yi – yeh…! yippee – yi – yoh…!"

This gets everybody going, especially Randy's fancy piece who is sitting down front looking up at her hero and joining in with the chorus, like. She's knocking back the old mother's ruin like there's no tomorrow and smoking herself silly, ain't she?

"Yippee – yi – yeh…! Yippee – yi – yoh…! – Ghost riders in the sky…!"

"Did your wife like the bathroom unit, Mr Mayor?" I enquire, grateful for the favour he's done me with the BBC. But would you believe it? The old sod's nodding off to sleep just sitting there, ain't he? Often does it though, a habit I'm told he has. Come to think of it I remember him doing the very same thing at me old school with the opening of our new swimming pool there last year. I think he'd been drinking down the Club prior to attending the function. He just drops off, like, snores an'all. Bit embarrassing for his wife who was speaking at the time, ain't she? Still, they managed to wake him in time for the cutting of the tape ceremony. Was quite an event really. I mean, a secondary-mod having their own swimming pool! Made a few of them other schools jealous, you know. Specially those private ones, wot! Some of them ain't even got a pool. Both me and Carol were at the opening. We all sat in the main hall together before trooping off over to the new pool to witness the ceremony. Quite a few other ex-pupils were in attendance also, along with the many mums and dads. Good luck to the kids is what I say. I mean, we had to walk to the town centre for a school swimming period, didn't we? Must be nice having one so handy for them now. It's also open to the public in the evenings and weekends, so all us swimming enthusiasts are well pleased, ain't we? Me and Carol used to go quite frequently, both being pretty good swimmers. I'm going to miss this recreation now that she's taken up with Tarp.

The mayor arouses from his semi-slumber to answer me question, don't he? "Yes... yes..." he mumbles with some embarrassment. "Very pleased, Henry, lad – wife's very pleased with it – very pleased."

"That's good," I declares, happy to hear it.

"Yippee – yi – yeh...! Yippee – yi – yoh...! Ghost riders in the sky...!" Randy finishes his song amid wild applause from an enthusiastic audience

. By this time the beer's really flowing, ain't it? And everybody's really enjoying themselves. Straight away Randy goes in to his next number, his whip cracking noisily and his gun blazing. His young woman is still putting the gins away and gazing up at her Saturday night hero with a look of sheer admiration showing in her glazed blue eyes.

The mayor suddenly comes to life with a start. "Bloody hell!" he gasps, groping desperately for his cigar that has fallen from his stubby little fingers down between his short, fat legs somewhere. There's cigar ash all down the front of the jacket of his dark suit. With considerable effort he finally manages to locate the offending object and wedges it securely between his thin lips in the corner of his twisted mouth once more. You see, our mayor's a small geezer with rather a large head on narrow shoulders. He's also balding, has red bloodshot eyes and a nose the colour of a flashing Belisha beacon, don't he? "Bloody hell!" he exclaims again, gazing about him, a bewildered look showing on his tired clown-like face. "Bit bloody noisy in here, ain't it?"

My old man finishes his beer, wiping his mouth with the back of his hand. "Yeah, it's that bloody cowboy up there," he says irritably, getting to his feet. "Let's have another drink, to obliterate the sound, shall we?"

So we all drinks up and gets a refill. Shortly after this, old Randy Bates comes over to our table and congratulates me on getting the BBC audition, don't he? Seems the mayor's been telling a few people what he's done for me, like. News soon gets about. Let's hope I can make something of it. The compere leaps on stage again. "Little piece of info just come my way, ladies an' gents! Seems our Henry is going to London for an audition with the BBC in a couple of weeks' time! How about that!"

The news is met with loud round of applause from everyone present.

"I'm sure you'd all like to join me in wishing him all the best for this wonderful opportunity! Good luck to ya, Henry!"

More applause, along with whistles. Hooray for bleeding Hollywood!

"Now is as good a time as any for our Henry to give us a sample of his music… don't you think, folks?"

"Yeah – come along, Henry!" everyone agrees.

Me mum and dad is joining in with the chanting also, ain't they? So I finds meself up on stage again with me guitar to give them all a taste of me musical repertoire, like. I sing them a number what I've recently finished composing. Oh, yeah – I'm a bit of a song writer as well, see. Nothing elaborate, mind. I just gets a tune going in me head, and when it's ready to come out, I play it on me guitar with a tape recorder running. I adds words to it afterwards. Done quite a few numbers in this way, I have. Never sung any of them in public 'till now though. Double-Cross-Baby, it's called. They seemed to like the song very much after I've performed it.

So I'm well pleased with the way things is going for me really, ain't I? It seems I got everyone rooting for me. Except Carol, of course. Am really sorry about this. I didn't realise I could miss someone so much. I've not seen anything of her since our bust up, have I? Course, I bump into her at work; but she has nothing to do with me now, does she? Seems to be this barrier between us. She's still knocking around with Tarp, so I suppose in her own mind she's well rid of me. Pity, cos I still reckon we could make a go of it meself. God! When I think of the times we've had together. I mean, it's not every weekend that we'd spend at the Labour Club, is it? See, I've got a car – right old banger really. Well, me and Carol might travel different places in it, mightn't we? Up to London sometimes, or just plain driving around our town, like. Mind – that's not as easy as it sounds these days, I can tell you. Great deal of road development, etc., is going on here in Wufton, see. Like in most towns we have a Town Hall, naturally. Well, they've just recently completed a huge underpass and roundabout complex system here. Strangers just get plain lost when trying to find some place or other in Wufton now, you know. I mean, instead of an ordinary straight forward roundabout as it used to be with grass lawns and verges and flower-beds and everything... well, that's all gone. We're left instead with a bleeding great concrete canyon of sorts, with traffic zooming in all directions above directly outside the Town Hall, while below, bewildered pedestrians grope their way along tunnels hoping to eventually come out at the right exit. Talk about bleeding Colditz! I mean, you go in at one end hoping to emerge outside the public library at the other, only to find yourself landing up in the bloody supermarket instead. Right maize, it is. Still, that's progress for you. Least, that what we're told it is.

Anyway, like I say, me and Carol would visit all the places of interest to us on a Saturday night. Dances, movies, swimming, a few drinks. We liked to go ice skating as well. We're pretty good skaters, see. You can imagine the fun we had. Dancing at Wufton Town Hall was another one of our pastimes. And then afterwards in the car... or perhaps at her place, or mine maybe. Didn't matter which, because both our parents would be down the Labour Club enjoying themselves. Yeah, we would get down to the lovey-dovey bit then, wouldn't we? We'd get carried away sometimes, and it'd be all we could do to keep control of our emotions, like. Not that we didn't wanna lose control. After all – only human, ain't we? Besides which, Carol's a very pretty gal with an exceptionally beautiful figure. Blonde hair, blue eyes, sweet face. Can she snog! Her hair hangs all long down her shoulders. She doesn't favour much make-up. Doesn't have to. Wears all the trendy gear. Wanna see what she does for a pair of jeans. Wow! She's a very easy going person. Lots of people get the wrong impression of her, thinking she's a gal of easy virtue. But nothing could be further from the truth. And I should know. She's a very sweet kid, and to be perfectly honest I'm still nuts about her really. That's why I'm so annoyed at Tarp stealing her away like he has. Using his position and money to impress her, ain't he? It can't possibly be anything else, can it? I mean, I hardly ever find Carol at home at evening these days. Each time I go round for her and do happen to find her in, she's either in the bath or else washing her hair or something. So we just don't see each other really. Trouble is, when a relationship such as ours breaks up it can affect other people as well, can't it? I mean, there's Carol's folks for a start. Don't see much of them now. Her dad don't go to the football anymore on a Saturday afternoon, and they hardly ever pop into the Club like they used to, do they?

"Why don't you and Carol make it up together?" me mum questions me over our meal.

"What's up, Son – had a lover's quarrel?" me dad wants to know.

"I mean, you've known each other since school days, haven't you?" me mum keeps on at me.

"Must admit, it won't seem right without young Carol around, Henry", me dad confesses.

"Surely the two of you can get together again, Son?" "What's she doing with herself these days, lad?"

And there's the answer staring right up at me from a column in the Wufton Gazette, ain't it? "Winning beauty contests by the bleeding looks of it," I informs them both of this piece of printed information.

Me mum takes the paper from me and begins reading: "Carol Shelley was voted this year's Carnival Queen of Wufton by a committee of officials at the Town Hall on Tuesday evening. The crowning ceremony will take place in the Town Hall at a later date. It is hoped that TV personality, Reggie Summers, of Up

Your Alley comedy series fame will be in attendance to crown this year's Queen."

"Well, I never!" me old man explains, rolling himself a fag. "Our Carol – who'd ever believe it!"

I didn't, for one, as I'm sitting there with me mouth half open with the news. So... this is what she's been up to lately? Parading around in the altogether in front of dirty old Town Hall officials? Makes you sick, don't it?

"She is a nice looking girl though, Henry," me mum comments, admiring Carol's photo in the paper.

"That she is," me old man agrees, lighting his fag.

"She's done herself proud winning the competition. Must have been hundreds of entries for it."

"Good luck to her is what I say," adds me dad, filling the room with Golden Virginia smoke.

I starts drinking me cuppa tea and heave a great big sigh. "Yeah- good bleeding luck to you, gal!"

I'm feeling sad at heart though and am as jealous as bloody hell really. Jealous of old Tarp being in a position he is to help Carol in this way. I mean, it don't give a normal bloke a chance, does it? But I mustn't let it get to me. After all, I'll be having my chance soon with the BBC, won't I? I'll bloody well show them what Henry can do, just see.

At present though I have got some spare time on me hands, ain't I? So I teams up with an old school mate – Spud Milligan – and we go out together for a spell. Seems Spud's broken with his latest bird, so we both got something in common there, ain't we? Nice bloke, Spud. Old man's a postman. Bloody good footballer, Spud, centre forward. The fifth form gals used to go a bomb on him, they did. They'd stand on the touch line cheering their hero on. Still plays the game for his work's team on Saturdays. Works at the paper factory. Could've had a job there meself; but I didn't fancy it. Shift work, see. Money's good. Lousy hours though. Anyhow, we goes out on the town a few nights together. We even manage to pull a couple of birds one Saturday night up at the Dance Hall, don't we? From the London estate, they were just up the rail from Wufton. All right, too; but I ain't really in the romancing mood, am I? So I split and leave Spud to it, like. He seems to have hit it off with his one. I dunno. What us blokes'll do for a bit of skirt, eh? Must be barmy. So that's the last I see of Spud's for a bit, ain't it?

In the meantime, I actually manage to speak a few words with Carol at work, congratulating her on her Carnival Queen winning and wishing her all the best on her big night at the Town Hall later in this merry month of May.

"Thank you, Henry – that's very sweet of you," she says to me from behind her desk in Tarp's office this particular morning in question. Seems Tarp's out somewhere on business. It's during our coffee break, so Carol asks me to sit down.

"It's all right… Mr Tarp won't be in till later this afternoon," she assures me, smiling her cute smile. "So – how have you been keeping, Henry?"

"Not so bad. How's yourself?"

"Yes, I'm fine, thanks."

We both sip our coffee as an embarrassing silence follows Then Carol suddenly asks, "That right about you and the BBC, Henry?"

All this while I'm dying to tell her the news, like, ain't I? But I don't rush things, finishing me coffee first, keeping the young lady in suspense.

"Oh, that," I finally replies in a matter a fact sorta way. "Yeah – I've got an audition with them next week, luv."

"That's just marvellous, Henry, it really is."

I must admit that Carol does sound excited about it all.

"I hope it goes well for you, I really do," she says kindly.

"Thanks, Carol – so do I."

She then reaches out for me hand across the desk. "No hard feelings, eh, Henry?"

I press her soft hand in mine. "No, of course not, luv," I answer.

"I've been missing you a lot," she confesses to me with sincerity.

I'm somewhat puzzled by this sudden affection she's showing me so I say. "Have you?"

I can't quite make her out. I mean, it was her that broke off our relationship, weren't it? Who the hell can figure women out, eh?

"I have, honest," Carol goes on in this way, still holding me hand. She then mumbles something about old Tarp and how I mustn't mistake their relationship together being something what it ain't. "After all, he's old enough to be me dad!"

"Course he is," I attacks quickly and hurtfully.

"Perhaps we could start again where we left off, Henry, when… well, when this is all finished?"

But now it's my turn to get me back up, ain't it? "What – when you've won your bleeding Carnival Queen crown and Tarp's no longer any use to you, gal? Is that what you're trying to say?" I spits venomously.

Carol's swift to withdraw her hand.

"That's what you really mean, isn't it, Carol?" I insist, the mood between us changing dramatically.

Carol makes no reply; but I can see she's boiling underneath. So I decide it's time I made an exit, like. Not before I add just one more home truth to the young lady first though. "You shouldn't use people, Carol! It's not nice."

"You better go, Henry," Carol requests, trying her utmost to control her temper.

"Don't worry – I am!" I shouts, striding out the office door toward me recluse the other side. Poor old Miss Pruce and old man Jenkins both shoot me bewildered looks, no doubt wondering what the hell's going on.

But I ask you – Carol in there – who the hell does she think she is? Trying to make it up with me after using Tarp the way she has? Probably thinks I'll make a go of it as a pop singer and now finds it more of an attraction than mixing with old Town Hall officials and ageing lavatory merchants, ain't it? Surely not though? I mean, Carol never used to be like this. Gosh! When I think of that time we had down at Southend. Hell! You wouldn't think it was the same girl. Different altogether she was then. I remember the outing very well. Think everyone did really. Lovely warm day with the sun shining throughout. We left Tarp's yard about eight-thirty in the morning, all the office crowd and workers aboard the coach hired for this occasion. Tarp came along, reading his bleeding *Daily Telegraph* all the way down to the coast. We arrived shortly after ten, so we all had plenty of time in which to enjoy ourselves before returning to the coach at the arranged time of ten o'clock that night. Course – everyone splits once we arrive, don't they? Naturally, meself and Carol goes off together. I also notices old man Jenkins and Miss Pruce pairing up with each other. Who knows – perhaps the old devils are having a wild passionate affair? Be a laugh, wouldn't it? Stranger things happen though. Don't know whose company Tarp finishes up with – not that I'm particularly interested anyway. All I know is that me and Carol are to spend the whole day together.

And what a day it turned out to be. We start by taking a stroll along the front gazing about us at everything and everyone. Surprising how many people there was around so early in the day. Like us, I suppose – coach trip outings from up and down the country. Pop'lar place – Southend. I quite like the resort meself. Mind, that's cos I ain't never been anywhere else really. Even so, I still reckon and believe you can have just as good a time here as some of those other bleeding places on the continent.

The tide's in, so we sits on this wall arm in arm down by the pier looking out to sea. It's a beautiful clear day and we can see for miles. Numerous boats are bobbing about at various points on the water, while further out a large tanker ploughs its way slowly out to sea.

There's crowds scattered right along the stretch of beach, some of them in swimming gear, some just plain sitting back in their deck- chairs sunning themselves. A soft breeze is blowing, and I feel a thrill surge through me, like, at the sight of Carol's lovely fair hair blowing about in it.

Then she looks at me with her beautiful blue eyes and says, "Let's have a nice day today, Henry."

I pulls her closer to me. "'Course we will, Carol," I answer, feeling very happy just sitting there with her on the wall, like. "What you wanna do first, luv?"

Before answering she leans over and gives me a lingering kiss full on the lips, don't she? "We'll do the works, shall we?" she then says hurriedly. "We can start by visiting the fortune teller…

Always wanted me fortune told. Then go for a drink some place along the front... Have us a meal. Oh, I wanna travel along the pier on the train – that's a must, Henry."

"If you say so, darlin'."

We're sitting there all cosy, like, ain't we? And I don't want this happy feeling with Carol ever to end.

"Wanna turn on the Big Wheel, too, Henry... And the Haunted House. We can spend a lot of time at the fairground. I love fairs. Then in the evening we can come down here to sit on the beach and watch the sun set before going for a final drink and the coach home." We sit thinking about all these wonderful things we're going to do, while the sun beats down on us and the sea laps gently in and out right along the beach in front of us until we eventually jumps down from the wall and begins walking along the front again.

"Pubs are open, luv!" I comment, noticing one close by with numerous people standing and sitting about outside drinking and chatting in the sunshine. "Fancy a glass?"

"Why not – get us off in a good mood, won't it?"

We enter the Bar and I order a cool beer while Carol plumps for a gin and tonic with ice. We sit in the corner out of the way to gaze romantically into each other's eyes.

"Wonder what the others are up to?" Carol then asks, lighting a cigarette.

"Oh, I s'pose Tarp's busy getting himself drunk somewhere, I don't think?"

"Be a laugh, that would."

A few drinks later and after I've just returned from paying the loo a visit, Carol suddenly indicates that she wants to leave the place, don't she? She seems upset about something. Her pretty face is all flushed, like.

"What's up, luv?" I ask after we've hurried outside.

"Bloke in the pub..." she begins to explain.

"What about him?"

"Exposed himself, didn't he?"

"What you talking about – exposed himself?" We're hurrying along the front at a rare old pace.

"When you were out in the toilet," Carol pants, "this bloke... this geezer. Like I say... Came right up to me with it in his hand..."

I grabs Carol by the arm, bringing her to a halt. We're right outside the candy floss stand, ain't we? "Would you mind explaining yourself, luv? Now... what exactly happened? Drink ain't gone to your head, has it?"

But I can see by the look on her face that Carol is deadly serious in her accusations, like.

"Surely this nutter just didn't walk up and flash himself at you, did he?"

"Yes, he did... That's just exactly what he did do." Carol gathers herself together. "So – I didn't know what to do, did I?"

"Did... did he say anything?"

"No – he just walks... straight up to me and asks if I like what I sees, don't he?"

"What did you say?"

"Nothing. What was I supposed to say? Didn't know what to do, did I? Didn't know where to put me face neither. Bloody embarrassing, I can tell you."

She pauses for breath, hurriedly lighting herself a cigarette. Then, puffing away at it frantically continues: "Having me on though, weren't he?"

"Watcha mean?" I asks, highly amused by it all really. I mean, fancy just coming up to somebody in a pub and flashing it, like? Not on, is it?

"'Cos the wretched thing drops off on the floor, don't it?"

It's more than I can take, I tell you. "What's up – did he have knob rot?" I jokes, bursting with laughter.

"No – the thing's made of plastic, ain't it?"

"Plastic?"

We resumes our walk along the front.

"Seems you can buy these items in the sex shops. Least, that's what this girl who's with him tells me, don't she?"

We stroll along in silence for a while. Then I says: "I dunno – what next? Sex bleeding shops! What's the world coming to?"

"Search me," Carol replies more calmly now, seeming to be over her shock. "Embarrassing though for a young girl. Wonder what you would have done in my place, Henry?"

"Chucked it out the window, gal – that's what!" I jokes.

Carol throws her cigarette away and links her arm in mine. "Oh, come on – let's go enjoy ourselves."

"Yeah – lets," I say as we stride toward the funfair together.

And what a time we had there. We goes on just about everything... Dodgems, Helter-Skelter, Ghost Train, Haunted House, Big Wheel, Switchback. The Big Wheel gives me tummy a bit of a turn, mind; but I eventually recover, like. We have a right giggle inside the Haunted House, and between laughs we kiss and cuddle each other, don't we? It was hilarious with the funny shaped mirrors. All shapes and sizes, ain't we?

Afterwards, we goes for some fish and chips in one of them Fish Bars along the front. Lashings of salt and vinegar. Delicious! "Come on, Henry – let's catch the train along the pier!" Carol says excitedly when we've finished eating.

So this is what we do, ain't it? Sitting ourselves in one of them small carriages they have and holding hands. Surprising how many folks like to do this. The train's packed solid. We sit looking out the window either side of us at the sea which is going out with the tide at the moment in the distance. Great view, like. At the end of the pier we buy a stick of rock each to take back with us.

"Having a nice time, Henry?" Carol enquires as we step down from the train on completing our excursion.

"Marvellous, thanks, luv," I replies, chewing me peppermint rock.

"Fancy a look round that Spanish Galleon?" She points at the ship in question which is anchored just by the pier.

"Yeah – why not?" I takes her hand and whisks her aboard the pirate vessel. Ho, ho, me hearties!

We have a close look round, especially at the various waxwork effigies of seamen below deck depicting their captivity and torture.

After this we goes on a pub crawl. Carol's all the while on the lookout for geezers flashing themselves; but we don't see any, do we? Just as well I suppose, cos it ain't very nice, is it? I mean, even I would be embarrassed at the sight of someone doing this.

Then Carol remembers the fortune-teller, don't she? "Nearly forgot, Henry," she says to me. "Come on – must find one before we go back."

So we leaves the pub and starts looking for a Gypsy Rose bleeding Lee, don't we? It don't take long and I finds meself sitting in a darkened room with Carol while some old dear whose all dressed up for the part in baubles, bangles and beads starts examining the palm of Carol's delicate little hand. Right laugh really. I mean, as if anyone can tell your future in this way? Still, if it makes Carol happy, then why not? "This your young fella, me dear?" the old gal asks her, smiling across at me with smudged lipstick teeth.

"Yeah – going steady, ain't we, Henry?"

I mumbles that we are, and gives Carol a kick on the shin under the table in hopes she'll hurry up and finish with this crystal ball nut.

"Uhmm… Seems you two might be marrying soon… I can see a church spire…"

The old gal stops ranting for a moment to take a closer look at Carol's hand. "I can also see a baby! Yes – there's a baby all right. Planned for an early family, have you, me dearies?"

"No, we bleeding well ain't!" I explodes, jumping up to get the hell out of the place, like. "Least, not to my knowledge anyway."

Carol gets to her feet as well, obviously sensing my desire to leave. "Thanks very much," she mutters, paying the mystic lady her reading fee. "It's been most interesting."

I takes her by the arm and we makes a hurried exit.

"Bloody barmy!" I gives Carol my opinion of what's just taken place inside the gypsy's tent when we're outside in the sunshine once more.

Carol just stands there looking up into my eyes and smiling.

"What's so funny?" I asks.

She taps my nose affectionately with her finger. "Never know – the old dear might be right in her predictions, Henry? Perhaps we shall marry and have a baby one day?"

"Yeah – she might be wrong as well. Come on – let's go down on the beach."

Carol slips her arm through mine and we heads off.

We find a nice secluded spot in front of some coloured chalets perched high on the wall behind us. There's no one else around, the sun worshippers and swimmers having deserted the beach at this time of day.

"Glad you came today, Henry?" Carol asks, sitting close beside me on the pebbly beach.

"Course I am, luv," I answers, feeling pleasantly happy having her all to meself at long last. The soft breeze is still blowing, and the sea keeps rolling in and out with the incoming tide, gently lapping the stretch of beach in front of us. The old sun is slowly slipping down the sky like a huge-shining copper penny the other side of the water, like, and it really is a beautiful sight to behold.

"So am I," Carol confesses, lying back comfortably on the beach, her hands clasped behind her head as she gazes up at the clear sky above. "I've really enjoyed myself today, Henry. 'Specially the Big Wheel – that was great."

I leans back beside her and informs her again that I've had a swell time too, Then, before I really knows what's happening, Carol's suddenly rolled over on top of me and is kissing me, ain't she? "Oh, Henry," she pants in me ear, "I want us to… to…"

"To what, Carol?" But I know perfectly well what she wants us to do, don't I?

"Will… will you make love to me, Henry?"

I gives her a lingering kiss, then offers: "If… if you're really sure that's what you want, darlin'?"

"Well, we have been going steady since schooldays, haven't we, Henry?"

"We most certainly have," I agree with her statement, which of course is perfectly true.

"And not once have we put a foot wrong, have we, Henry?"

"Not once, Carol, no," I answers, getting all excited as I starts slipping her jeans off.

"And we will be careful, won't we, darling?" Carol is panting between passionate kisses. Her voice betrays her nervousness, conscious of the fact that after years of courting we were at last on the verge of making love together.

These are the last words spoken on the subject until Carol rolls off me after we've gone through the motions of the wonderful act of making love right there on the beach. It really was beautiful, and we just lay there afterwards looking up at the sky. But then we both get the urge to do it again, so I lay on top of her this time, and we go through the motions yet once again. As I say, it really was beautiful. *So* beautiful.

"Oh, Henry!" murmurs Carol, caressing me with her soft hands.

"Carol!" I utters, a feeling of fulfilment, contentment, surging through me.

And that's how we end our wonderful day at Southend, ain't it? Pity our romance has since ended, like. Seems such a shame when two people who used to get on so well together should now find this relationship no longer exists. But there it is. Carol's now got her head full of winning beauty competitions and is mixing with Tarp and the likes of his bleeding lot, ain't she? Be interesting to see where it all leads really, won't it?"

Chapter 3

Not that I ain't got plenty to do, like, just cos I'm not seeing Carol anymore. I mean, I got me audition coming up this Friday, so I'm busy preparing for this, ain't I? I'm also going up me old school twice a week to rehearse for a Show that the Parents and Teachers Association is putting on at the Town Hall in another month's time. Not that I'm a parent, like, or indeed a teacher. I've just been asked by them to participate in their production, that's all. Plus the fact that I enjoy doing it tremendously. I'll probably bump into Carol because of it cos as you know she's getting crowned Carnival Queen that night. Should be good fun – the Show, I mean. Least, if the rehearsals are anything to go by, that is. It's a cabaret type concert. In fact it is actually called Cabaret, with a cast of about twenty performing in it. Musical director is a teacher at the school, while the secretary of the association is producing the package. Some of the teachers are also playing in the band as well. In aid of the old folk in this area it is – senior citizens – you know? Their annual big night out.

So you can see I'm quite a busybody really. But what I'm all keyed up about though is this coming Friday in London with the BBC, ain't it? Wonder how I shall fair out? Should be all right. Just do me best is all that I can do really.

Anyway, things back at the office are much the same with Carol still seeing plenty of old Tarp, like. I did hear that the geezer's taking her out for a night on the town after she's been crowned at the old folks Show. All right for some, ain't it? Still, if this is what she really wants – then good bleeding luck to her. Hardly seems possible though that me and her... well, making love like we did down on the sand at Southend? We hardly say a word to each other now, do we? Funny old world we live in, ain't it?

So me and the folks pops round to the local pub sometimes when we ain't paying the Labour Club a visit, like, to have a few drinks.

"Yes, it's our Henry's big day tomorrow at the BBC," me mum says to the landlord's missus the night before this occasion. "Hope he doesn't get lost on them underground trains though?"

The old man gets the beers in and we sits down for a quiet night's drinking. S'not much of a pub, our local; but there are some right real characters that use the place. All bleeding sorts, I can tell you.

"Good luck tomorrow, Henry!" Tony Smalls wishes me, standing with his elbow resting on the bar counter. Tony's recently gone in to the coal humping business, ain't he? Bought himself an old truck and is doing very nicely for himself, I do believe. He can't go far wrong really, what with the whole of the estate being on coal central heating since this here recent modernisation, like.

"Thanks, Tony," I acknowledge him. "How's the coal racket doing then?"

"Yeah, all right, mate. Anytime you want some cheap – just give us a nod, Henry, okay?"

"I'll certainly keep you to that."

Handy having such mates, I tell you. 'Specially with the winter months yet to come, like.

The doors of the pub swing open, admitting a small, heavily lined faced geezer into the bar who's known to all as Stench cos of his rather obnoxious body aroma.

"Come on!" he shouts, chewing the end of his roll-up as he pushes his way up to the bar. "Make way! Make way! Let a hard working bloke get himself a drink."

"Hello, Stench," Tom Bassett, the landlord greets the guy. "How's things?"

"Could be better, Tom – could be better."

"Get away – the richest bloke in here tonight… Ain't that right, fellas?"

"No!" a chorus of voices disagree with this from one end of the bar.

"*You* are!" they shout.

"'Bout time he bought us all a bleeding drink then, ain't it?" Stench hollers.

But the landlord don't say nothing, like – just quietly keeps pulling pints for his thirsty customers, don't he? Still, I wouldn't mind betting he is worth a few bob, like. Makes a few quid on the side does our Tom, I know. Aside from the profits him and his missus makes on lunches, there's also the Disco's he runs every Thursday night upstairs. Really popular, these are. All the kids turn out for them. Went to a couple meself, like. Flashing lights and everything. But I stopped going when fights starts breaking out. Don't hold with that sort of thing. Tom hired a bouncer to sort out some of these hard nuts. Great big bloke who goes by the name of Basher. Should see him when he goes into action. Wouldn't like to mix it with him, I tell you.

I've been told though that he's a quiet bloke at heart. Seems that's all he does for a living – bouncing. Just two or three dances a week and he's earned himself a fair old screw. Got a lovely place of his own apparently. Just shows what a bit of brawn can do for you, don't it?

So old Stench gets his drink and sits himself down in the corner.

Standing next to him and propping up the bar is a character by the name of Jason, a middle-aged geezer with a Clark Gable type appearance and who speaks with a phoney American accent. "Frankly, my dear, I don't give a damn!" No one knows why he does this – never been to the U S of A in his bleeding life, has he? He's not a bad bloke at heart though. Bit of a hard nut in his day – even served time in the jug for doing some bloke over.

"Gee – seems to be a strong smell this end of the bar all of a sudden, Ta...rm," he drawls. Then, making out he's just seen the new arrival, explains: "Oh – it's you, Stench. Explains it then, don't it, fellas?"

And that's how the conversation is most evenings in our local. As I says, we gets all sorts in, but the majority is all hard working guys and dolls – the true working class of our society, you might say. The old mayor likes to pop in now and again just to see how everything is, like. And there's another counsellor geezer what frequents the place also. Does a lot of hard graft for the Labour Party, he does.

"What you having to drink, Will?" me old man asks the mayor on this particular night in question.

"I'll have a wee scotch, Charlie, if I may," he requests. "How's everything for tomorrow, Henry, lad?" he then asks me, lighting himself a cigar.

"Fine, thanks, Mr Mayor," I replies, sipping me brown ale.

"I don't like him travelling on them underground trains, I don't," me mum interrupts.

"I'm telling you he'll be all right, woman," me dad assures her, arriving back at our table with Will's drink.

"Yes, I'm sure he will," the mayor agrees.

None of this is bothering me to that extent, for I sincerely believe that I'll be fine and that I'll do well at the audition. I knows what number I'm gonna do, like, and I have me own backing on me guitar sorted, ain't I? I'll give it my best shot and hope that those BBC geezers like what I have to offer. Who knows – I might just get to be famous overnight and will be able to knock me silly old job at Tarp's on the head because of it?

Anyway, the mayor's just getting the drinks in before the last bell, when who do you think walks in to the bar, only Carol, don't she? Comes straight over to our table and says to me: "Hello! Henry. Just popped in on my way home to wish you all the best for tomorrow."

I sits looking up into her lovely blue eyes, like, don't I? God! She looks beautiful, and the sight of her brings a lump to me throat. "Thanks, Carol," I answers, appreciating this gesture on her part.

"Have yerself a drink, lass?" the mayor offers, placing our glasses on the table.

"No – no thanks. I've Mr Tarp waiting outside in the car for me."

This piece of information immediately gets me back up, don't it? I mean – I notice he don't come in to wish me luck, does he? Still, the old sod's given me the day off with full pay, so I suppose I shouldn't expect too much, should I?

"Well – bye then, Henry," Carol says to me quietly. "I really do hope it goes well for you."

"Thanks, Carol," I responds with a deep sigh. "And thanks for coming in to see me, luv."

I watch as she disappears out through the door, and I start to feel all sad, like. You see, I'm still very fond of her. I only wish she was coming with me tomorrow. I mean, we're used to doing things together, ain't we? Seems a pity that with something as important as this she won't be there with me to share the experience. It would certainly give me more confidence, I know. At the moment though we seem to be travelling in opposite directions, don't we? That's life I suppose.

"Haven't you two made up together yet?" me dad enquires after she's left.

"You should, you know," me mum agrees, sipping her stout.

"Lover's quarrel, have you, lad?" the mayor enquires, dropping cigar ash all down the front of his grey suit.

I heaves another sigh. "Yeah – you could say," I says sadly, thinking about our time down at Southend together. God! We were happy then all right. Could we be again?

"Been seeing a lot of that Mr Tarp, ain't she?" me mum comments with obvious disapproval.

"Perhaps he fancies the young 'uns, eh?" me dad suggests jokingly.

"Get away – he's not a bad sort at heart, Charlie," the mayor comes to his defence, blowing smoke into the already smoke-filled room.

"You're only saying that 'cos he fitted you out with a new bathroom unit on the cheap, Mr Mayor," I remarks unkindly.

"Now, now, Henry – no need for that kinda talk. Show some respect for your elders, please," me dad scolds me.

"Especially after all the Mayor's done for you, Henry," Mum reminds me.

I finishes me beer. "I'm sorry, Mr Mayor. Slip of the tongue, I assure you."

The mayor stubs his cigar out in the glass ash tray on the table in front of him. "S'all right, Henry. No harm intended, I'm sure, lad."

"Time, gents, if you please!" the landlord suddenly shouts for the benefit of all present.

"All right, matey – keep your hair on," Stench retaliates by slowly finishing his drink.

Jason downs the remains of his and reaches for his leather jacket that's draped over the back of me old man's chair. "Good night to you all," he drawls.

As we make our way out of the bar the mayor wishes me all the best for the following day before we all goes our separate ways.

Once home, Mum makes us a hot chocolate drink. Then I calls it a day, like, and goes off up to bed.

"See you on the nine-thirty to Euston in the morning, Son!" me dad calls up after me. "And good luck to you, lad!"

Chapter 4

The next day finds me rising early to take a bath and shave before going down to a fried eggs and bacon breakfast that ma's been busy preparing.

"You all right, Henry?" she asks, pouring me a cuppa tea.

"Fine, thanks, Ma." I'm feeling happy. Not that I usually am on working days at this particular hour, mind. Today's different, though. No work. No Tarp. I mean – just the thought of him is enough to put the mockers on any bloody day, ain't it?

"Your Father's been out working since early – he's probably on his second run to London by now?"

I'm munching me fried bread.

Ma tops me cuppa up for me. "You will be careful today, won't you, Henry?

"I promise I will, Ma. Stop worrying so, will you?"

"Would hate to think of anything happening to you..."

"I'll be okay, I'm telling you."

I says me good-byes to her and leaves the house to walk the short distance to Wufton Junction. When I gets there, I pops into the cafeteria to say hello to old Rosy, don't I?

"Henry!" she greets me with a friendly smile. "How's things?"

It's great to see her smiling face and voluptuous boobs once again. "Yeah – I'm okay, thanks, Rosy," I informs her.

"Your big day at the BBC I hear – that right?"

"That's right, luv."

"Well – good luck to you, old fruit," she wishes me.

"Thanks a lot, Rosy." I really appreciate her kind gesture.

She's in the process of spooning sugar into the cups on the counter. I notices old Percy watching her every move from the far corner, unable to take his eyes off her.

"Made it up with Carol yet, Henry?" Rosy then enquires, slopping milk into the individual cups in front of her.

I swings me guitar up onto me shoulder. "No, no yet," I informs her sadly. I wish I could have told her otherwise; but there we are. Would have been lying, wouldn't I?

"Don't leave it too long, Henry – she won't wait forever you know?"

I hear what she says, but I don't answer, do I? After all, at the moment it looks like me and Carol won't be making it up together, don't it?

So I walks to the Station and climbs up the stairs to the platform where me train is waiting to pull out. Pa's made sure it's on time today, that's for sure.

"Everything all right, Son?" he asks from his position up front in his driving compartment as he catches sight of me walking toward him.

"Fine, thanks, Pa." I tells him, stepping into an empty compartment.

"Good luck to you then, Son,"

"Thanks – I'll give it me best, Pa."

I sits down in a seat in a carriage directly behind his control booth and then we slip slowly along the platform on our journey. En route I takes the opportunity to sing aloud the song I'm going to do at the audition.

"It's a double-cross, ba…by – it's a double-cross! Who'd ever thought you would double-cross! But I will get you, ba…by, yeah, I' gonna get you, ba…by – cos you ain't nothin' but a double-cross!"

Rather appropriate, this song, I reckon, don't you?

Arriving at Euston in good time I says farewell to me old man and heads for the busy streets of swingin' London Town. "It's a double- cross, ba…by – it's a double-cross!" I'm singing quietly to meself, trying to gain confidence for me big ordeal, like. I'm feeling a little nervous as I turns the corner and into the street and the building where the audition is being held. "But I will get you,

ba…by, yeah, I'm gonna get you, ba…by – cos you ain't nothin'
but a double-cross!"

"Name?" a tall geezer holding a clipboard and ticking off the
artists participating in this BBC gig, asks me as I enter a rather
crowded reception area.

"Higgins!" I informs him nonchalantly, in an effort to disguise
me nervousness. "Henry Higgins!"

After much checking that all arriving guests are accounted for,
this guy then gains everyone's attention by stating: "If you would
all like to enter the second door on your right down the corridor
here, please – thank you! Your names will be called when needed,
okay?"

We all move in the direction indicated and sit down to await
our turn. The first act to be auditioned is a young, heavily made-
up girl who commences to belt out a song in Shirley Bassey type
fashion with piano accompaniment. In fact if you didn't know it
was this gal, you'd think that Shirley Bassey herself was there in
person performing. Least, if the voice was anything to go by, you
bleeding well would, I know. Uncanny really.

"What sorta act are you into, sunshine?" a tall, young,
handsome- moustached bloke standing next to me and changing
in to a dickybow and dress suit, enquires.

"I'm a singer," I informs him, unzipping me guitar case. No
bloody dickybow for our Henry, is there? Just casual clothes –
jeans and sweater. I'm feeling real nervous now like, I can tell
you.

"Simon's the name – comedian," he introduces himself,
offering me his hand in friendship. "Simon Blackwell."

I returns his firm handshake. "Henry… Henry Higgins," I
inform him politely, happy to have someone to talk to. Helps
relieve the tension, don't it?

"Do it for a living?"

"What's that?"

"Caruso-ing? You know – singing?"

"No… Now and again at the Labour Club, that's all."

Simon adjusts his tie in front of a mirror on the wall.

"How about you?" I enquires tentatively.

"Christ no! A few regular bookings at weekends. Pubs mostly. Heh – hear the one about the Irishman that walks in to a flashy London restaurant?"

"No," I answer, taking an immediate liking to this smooth talking cockney.

"Well, he goes straight ahead and orders a first rate, first class meal from the menu. The lot – you know? Then – wait for it – he pays for it and walks right on out the place without eating it, don't he?"

His joke makes me chuckle, I must admit.

The Miss Bassey act concludes with a bang, everyone's ears suffering because of it. She's done her best though, ain't she? Even if she does lack originality.

"Simon Blackwell!" the geezer with the clipboard summons our comedian.

"Good luck then," I wishes him with sincerity.

"I'll see you later, Henry," he smiles at me cheekily before introducing himself with the utmost confidence to everyone.

"That's me, folks! – laugh a minute Simon," he jokes, jumping up onto the platform used as a stage. "Hold onto your seat-belts, cos here I am!"

I'm feeling a great deal more at home now, I must say. Makes all the difference if you've someone to relate to, don't it?

I'm next up to perform after Simon, as I steps out in front a panel of judges all seated at a table in front of me taking notes of the various acts as they see them. I'm asked if I want a pianist to accompany me, but I declines the offer. I work better on me own, see. 'Specially with me own material, like.

And so I sings me Double-Cross number whilst strumming me guitar, don't I? It goes pretty well after a nervous opening; but once I get really into the song I'm more than pleased with the finished product, I must say. When I'm finally through I'm told to wait behind, ain't I? Which sounds encouraging and perhaps indicates the panel's liking for my particular type of act.

"I see you made out all right then, kid?" Simon asks after I re-joins him. "You did well. Asked you to hang around, have they?"

"Yeah – seems so," I answers, feeling quite pleased with me effort. Over the moon really, ain't I? "How about you?"

"Same – they wanna see me."

While waiting we gets to chatting, don't we? I discover that Simon's a male model by profession.

"Money's good once you get in," he informs me enthusiastically. "Get to meet all kinds of people as well. Could do a lot worse, sunshine, I tell you. How about you – what line of business you in, Henry?"

Another act completes their turn, a conjuring clown as it happens, to make way for a guitar playing singing group, all with stars in their eyes and dreaming of overnight stardom no doubt.

"I work as a clerk for a bathroom and toilet accessories firm in Wufton," I admit to him dejectedly.

"Shit! Excuse the pun, like – but you wanna get out of that game, boy. No bread to be made there, I know. Fancy doing some modelling, Henry?"

"Don't know much about it," I confess above the noise of the pop group.

"You could learn from an agency training course. Get to know all the tricks of the trade, like."

"Sounds tempting, all right."

"Earn big bucks – television and everything. Fix you up with an interview if you like… I know this bloke, see?"

He hands me a calling card. "Give us a ring if you're interested, okay?"

"Okay, I will," I promises, slipping the card in me pocket.

We continue to chat until we notice that we are the only persons left in the room, everyone else having left after their auditions. 'Don't call us – we'll call you, eh?'

Then this tall geezer, trendily dressed and sporting a marvellous bloody suntan that he must have obtained from the beaches of sunny Spain or the likes, enters the room. A bead necklace is hanging from his rather long neck and rattling as he moves, as does a gold bracelet dangling from his wrist also. Should see him – a right looking ninny, ain't he? With a mop of fair, curly hair piled on top of his large bonce.

"Hello, dearies! I'm Brian Goodchild – television producer," he introduces himself. Man – you'd never believe it to look at him.

Meself and Simon looks at each other, hardly able to keep a straight face.

"We're in the throes of creating a new talent show at the moment." Goodchild lights up a cigar.

Then old Clipboard who is standing by his side, explains calmly:

"The show will be called 'Chance of a Lifetime' and is due to go out in about a month's time."

"We're looking for a couple of artists of your calibre to appear in it," Mr Baubles and Bangles adds, rolling his head from side to side.

"Mr Goodchild would like you both to appear in our little package- if you are interested, of course?"

Of course we are, ain't we? And we raises no objections to this here suggestion, both nodding our heads in agreement.

"Excellent!" Goodchild utters, chewing the end of his cigar. "Now – unbeknown to you I taped both your performances here today. You see, the general idea of the Show is to invite several unknown artists like yourselves along and then to inform a studio audience which one of you a panel of judges selects to be the winner of 'Chance of a Lifetime' at the close of the Show. Get the idea?"

"Roger and out," Simon jokes.

"Mr Goodchild has four other acts under consideration – so you won't actually know who the lucky winner is until the night of transmission," Clipboard informs us.

"Sounds fun," Simon says. Then, like a true good businessman that he undoubtedly is, he enquires: "I trust we get a fee for appearing on the box whether we've won the contest or not, do we?"

"Of course, dearies – plus your expenses," the producer explains. "Good – well, I think that about covers everything. If you would kindly give good Eric here a contact number for him to reach you we'll get in touch nearer the actual time and date of the Show. Look forward to seeing you both then, dearies, okay?"

And that's that. He vanishes through the door, rattling noisily on his way along the corridor outside. Eric follows suit after we've supplied him with our phone numbers. I'm thinking to meself what a surprise old Tarp will get once he finds out what's happening. 'Chance of a Lifetime' on bleeding BBC television, he'll never believe it, will he? But I'll show him. Carol, too. Just wait and see if I won't.

"Fancy a beer, Henry?" Simon asks, once we're outside in the street.

"Yeah – why not?" I replies, feeling happy at the way things have gone, like.

"May the best man win, eh, sunshine?" Simon comments after we've sat down in this pub just round the corner.

"That's right," I agree, sipping me beer.

Simon is quick to finish his drink, explaining that he has a modelling job to go to on the other side of London. "Don't forget – get in touch with me about that agency now?"

"Yeah, I think I will," I tells him.

"That-a-boy."

With that, he hands me this rather bulky envelope. "Take a gander at these, sunshine. 'Nuff to make your eyes water, some of 'em. You can return them when I next see you, okay?"

Then he's gone like a puff of smoke, ain't he? Must say I quite like the bloke – pleasant personality all right. I'm left feeling bewildered though as you can well imagine, wondering what's inside the package, like. So I empties the contents out onto the table in front of me... And what do you think? Photographs. Loads of 'em. Pornography! And some of them does make your eyes water, I can tell you. Should see them. Bloody hell! Is this what they call modelling then? But surely Simon's not mixed up in this sort of game? I dunno – life's certainly full of surprises, ain't it just?

I down another beer before leaving. Then, with me faithful guitar for company, I strides out on me journey towards the railway station, wondering whether I'll be the one lucky enough to win this 'Chance of a Lifetime' Show next month? Have to wait and see, won't we?

Chapter 5

In the meantime, though, it's back to work for Tarp at the office, with me catching occasional glimpses of Carol there. She's looking as lovely as always, while old Tarp, in sharp contrast, appears to me to be positively ugly and as miserable as ever. I'm thinking he could do with a charisma transplant, if indeed that was at all possible. But it would take a miracle for that ever to happen. Still, he does go out of his way to ask how me audition went.

"You never know – we might be watching you perform on telly one day, Higgins?" he manages to joke on his way through the office.

But it's Carol that's all excited by the news, ain't it?

"What was it like, Henry?" she asks enthusiastically. "What other acts were there? Do you think you might win? I'm ever so pleased for you, Henry, honest I am."

I think she genuinely is as well.

"How are things with you then, Carol?" I asks her one day when old Tarp's not in the office.

"I'm fine thank you, Henry," she answers, her bright eyes sparkling, her long, fair hair hanging all lovely down over her shoulders, making me feel excited at just the sight of her. Know what I mean?

"I s'pose you're looking forward to your Carnival Queen crowning?"

"Uhmm… very much."

"I'll be there on the night – Cabaret – the school Show, you know?"

"Yes, I know, Henry. By all accounts it should be a good one?"

49

"Yeah, it's coming along. As they say – should be all right on the night."

Suddenly our fingers touch across the desk, don't they?

"I've missed not being with you, Henry," Carol declares, giving me hand a squeeze.

"I've missed you, too, luv," I confesses truly to her.

"Do you think we might… well?"

"Make up, you mean?"

"Yes. What do you think?"

"I dunno – depends – don't it?"

"On what?"

"On priorities."

She looks at me for a moment all innocent, like. And do you know what? I could quite easily have kissed her, I felt that tempted to. But something prevents me from doing so, don't it?

"What do you mean by priorities, Henry?"

I clears me throat in preparation for what I'm about to say to her. A few home truths as a matter of fact. "Well, it all depends what it is you're actually after, luv, don't it?"

"What on earth do mean?" Carol questions me, her pretty face betraying a complete look of bewilderment.

"Well, do you want the high life with old Tarp here, or would you be prepared to jog along with me and what I'm involved in at the moment?"

Carol remains silent for a while. Then, still holding tight to my hand, utters: "Well, of course I want what you want, Henry. I've already told you not to get the wrong impression regarding Mr Tarp. There's absolutely nothing going on between us – and as for that day at Rosy's – well, I was in rather a bad mood, wasn't I?" She stops to regain her breath before continuing. "And as for me ranting about getting on in life and all that nonsense… well, I'm sure you'll do well in whatever you eventually choose to do, Henry. Anyway – I like you just the way you are, honest I do. Just so long as we can make up again is all I really want, luv. Just like old times, eh?"

I gazes deep into her blue eyes, and this time temptation proves too much for me, don't it? So I leans over and kisses her full on the lips.

"Oh, Henry," she murmurs, pulling me down until I'm nearly lying on top of her across the desk right there in bleeding Tarp's office.

Then what do you think happens? Yeah, you've guessed – old Tarp suddenly walks in on us, don't he?

"What's the meaning of this, Higgins?" he demands an explanation. Bloody furious, that's for sure, ain't he?

I quickly move off the desk and gets to me feet, adjusting me state of dress. "Well…!" I gasps; but I'm lost for words, ain't I? What's he expect? Silly old sod! What the hell's he come barging in for like that, for God's sake?

But Carol comes to me rescue, don't she? "It's not entirely Henry's fault, Mr Tarp. You see…"

But Tarp cuts her short. "Disgraceful! Absolutely bloody-well disgraceful! Such behaviour – and right here in my office of all places! What on earth do you think you are playing at, Higgins?"

"It was my fault, Mr Tarp – honest," Carol pleads in my defence, like.

"Will you please keep out of this, Carol," Tarp shouts at her.

"Don't you dare bleeding well talk to her like that," I hollers at him.

"Are you addressing me by any chance, Higgins?"

"You bet I am, you silly old sod!"

Tarp just stands there looking at me, at a loss for words himself for a change.

"And you can stick your perishing job an'all," I tells him defiantly, in a right old temper be now, like. "Stick it right up yer jacksy, mate!"

With this final statement from yours truly I storms off out the office. I'm raging, I tell you. To hell with his lousy job anyway. I'll get in touch with Simon and he can get me fixed up in the modelling profession.

Of course, Carol comes round my place later that evening, don't she?

"Are you really leaving Tarp's, Henry?" she asks with a certain amount of concern after me ma and pa have popped down the local for a drink.

"You bet I am, gal," I tells her straight. "Had enough. Going into modelling, ain't I?"

"You're not serious, surely?"

"I most certainly am. Why don't you have a go at it? I mean, you are this year's Carnival Queen, after all is said and done, ain't you?"

"What's that got to do with it, may I ask?"

"Nothing really... Just thought you might be interested, that's all. You could make a name for yourself?"

Carol looks at me for a while, then says quietly: "Perhaps I don't wanna make a name for myself, Henry."

Women! Who the hell can figure them out?

"Thought that's what you wanted... To get on and everything? 'Don't wanna spend the rest of your life selling bleeding lavatory pans, do you?' you says to me – remember?"

"I've already explained that bit, Henry." She pauses, obviously scheming up something inside her tiny little head. "Honest, Henry – that's not what I want."

It's my turn to think now, ain't it? "What do you want then, Carol?" I demands an answer from her.

She looks at me, then smiles sweetly. "Promise you won't laugh?"

"I won't – I promise."

She hesitates for a moment; but then jumps in with both feet, don't she? "I wanna get married – settle down, Henry," she surprises me with.

I gets up off the sofa we've been sitting on and stands looking down at her. I mean – just cos we've made love together on the beach down at Southend, don't give her any right to expect marriage now, does it?

"You must be jokin', gal!" I gasps, flabbergasted at her suggestion, like.

"No, I'm not," Carol replies in all seriousness.

"You're far too young for that sorta thing yet, Carol," I lectures her as if I'm some kind of authority on this particular subject. Then, as an afterthought, I asks: "I s'pose you've someone in mind, have you, luv?"

She, too, rises to her feet now, slipping her arms round me neck.

"Can't you guess, Henry?"

I manoeuvres me way out of her clutches. I likes the gal, sure – but Christ! No, I ain't nowhere near ready for marriage yet, am I?

"No, thanks," I declines her offer. "I wanna see a bit more of life before thinking along those lines, Carol."

Carol gives me a disappointed look. I mean, what gal wouldn't feel let down after having been refused a proposal of marriage now?

She grabs her bag from off the sofa. "Obviously you don't feel the same way as I do for you, Henry?" she grimaces, trying her hardest to hold back the tears from her eyes.

I can see she's hurting deeply. "I…I like you a hellava lot, Carol," I sympathises with her. "But as I've told you – I ain't ready for that sorta commitment yet, am I?"

But by now she's giving me the water works bit, ain't she? "S'all right, Henry," she sniffles. "No need to explain… I understand perfectly."

And with that she walks out of the room, closing the door quietly behind her.

Naturally, I feels sorry for her; but after all – there's nothing like frightening a bloke off, is there? I mean – marriage! S'not on, is it?

Anyway, I finally hands me notice in at Tarp's place, don't I? Then I gets in touch with Simon, who immediately arranges this interview for me with this here School of bleeding Charm in London.

So I goes up there the next day to see this geezer. I manages to get enrolled straight away on one of their courses to commence this following Monday, like. Apparently there's gonna be twelve other star-struck hopefuls taking part on this course also. There's ten lessons altogether, in which time they hope to teach us all about deportment, grace and bleeding charm, don't they? Then, with any luck, we should be fully fledged male models with all the various agencies clamouring for our services. Well – you never know – and as old Simon says – "There's money in it, sunshine!"

While I'm in London I returns Simon's package to him, don't I? Just in case you are wondering what's become of these here photos, like. Know what I mean?

"How did you make out, Henry?" Simon asks when we've gone for a coffee round the corner in this Milk Bar.

"They want me to start Monday," I informs him proudly. "I'm looking forward to it."

"That's good. What did you think of me picture postcards then?"

"Bit tasty, some of 'em, ain't they?"

"Yeah, you could say so."

He lights up a fag, gulps some of his coffee, giving me the distinct impression that he's got plenty of surplus energy, the way he's continually moving about, shifting. Know what I mean?

"It's nice seeing you again, Henry," he says, his hands gesticulating above the table in front of him and in danger of knocking things over.

"It's nice to see you, Simon," I answers him truthfully. I quite likes the bloke, see.

"Looks like we'll be seeing more of each other now, don't it?"

"Yeah. I've jacked me job in. Couldn't stand it no longer."

"Good for you, sunshine! You won't regret it. You'll see."

He stubs his cigarette out in the ashtray. "By the way, Henry – how do you fancy moving in with me at my place up at Harrow? Got a flat there, ain't I? Share the rent – what do you say?"

I finishes me coffee. "I – I dunno," I answers dubiously. "See what me parents think, eh?"

"Won't mind, will they?"

"Shouldn't think so."

"You've got me number. Give us a tinkle if you fancy the idea. It'll be nice having you."

"I'll let you know, okay?"

"Sure thing. Must go now... Regent's Park – shooting a chocolate commercial there this afternoon. I'll see you around then, Henry."

And he vanishes, don't he?

So I says me good-byes to everyone at Tarp's and departs from their lives. It's sad in one way; but I know it's for the best if

I'm intent on making a go of things, don't I? Even if it all don't go in my favour, it's better than hanging on there like old Miss Pruce or Mr Jenkins now, I know? Bless their little hearts really – salt of the earth, ain't they? I just don't fancy doing what they are when I'm their age, do I?

Of course, me old man thinks I'm daft, don't he? "Male bloody model?" he explodes when I've told him of me future plans, like.

"What exactly is it you'll be doing, Henry?" Ma enquires with her usual trepidation. I'm sure she thinks I'll be doing something immoral.

She's none the wiser after I've explained it to her.

"Taking a bit of a risk you know, lad," Pa says, filling the room with cigarette smoke. "Not many make it at that game, I know?"

"And what's all this about you sharing a flat with someone?" Ma wants to know.

It takes me quite some considerable time to explain to her about Simon and everything; but I don't think she's particularly happy with the sound of this set up, is she?

"What about Carol, Son? What's to become of her?"

"Haven't you two made it up together yet then?"

So it's another five minutes explaining me and Carol's present circumstances, ain't it?

"After all said and done, it's only natural that a young girl should want to settle down and marry and have a family, Henry?"

"Cos it is," the old man agrees with her statement. "No need to rush into it – she'd wait for you, lad, I'm sure of it."

But by now I've had enough, ain't I? "Look!" I says sternly to the pair of them. "I've made up my mind to go through with this. I'm sorry if it don't meet with your approval, like; but it is my life we're talking about here, and I would like some say in what I wanna do with it. So if you don't mind…"

The old man sees that I means business, don't he? And he backs off.

"All right, all right, Son," he says finally, going over to turn on the telly. "Far be it for me to stand in your way. Just keep in touch with your Ma from time to time is all we ask, okay?"

I'm thankful he's seeing reason. "I promise I'll keep you both informed of me welfare, won't I?" I assures them.

And that's that then, ain't it? All cut and dried. I even pays Carol a visit to say good-bye to her the night before me departure into the wide world. She wishes me all the best and we parts on good terms. I'm glad about this, cos it don't do to injure one another with heated words now, does it? Besides, we've had some pretty good times together. There's always those to remember, ain't there?

Chapter 6

So I moves in with Simon up at his place in Harrow, don't I? Small pad, but nice and cumfy and big enough for the two of us. It don't take me long to settle in, and would you believe it – we gets on like a house on fire. Not that we sees a great deal of one another to begin with. I mean, Simon's busy with his work during the daytime, ain't he? We get together at weekends mostly – that's if he's not chatting the birds-like. Great romancer is our Simon, you know. Different one each bleeding night. Italian, Spanish – you name it, Simon has 'em. The first Saturday I'm there, he throws a party, don't he? Bloody hell! Wanna see the crumpet that's present. From the modelling profession, most of them. A great time is had by all, with music playing practically all night. I'm introduced to loads of people which includes a couple of geezers what might be able to help me. In the modelling game, ain't they? By the way, I've been attending this School of Charm a couple of times a week since arriving at Simon's, ain't I? You'd never believe it – some bloke there has me walking up and down a catwalk with a book perched on top of me head, don't he? Trying to teach me grace and balance, like. It's a right laugh really. But it's all in the line of duty they tell me. If me folks could only see me now – they'd have fifty fits, I'm sure. Laugh their bleeding heads off, wouldn't they? But if this is what it takes to break in to the big time, then so be it. They teach me other things as well as the course progresses, like how to behave in front of a TV camera, how to wear clothes to show them off to their best advantage. Who knows? Perhaps I may turn out to be a chat show host. Well, somebody's got to do it, ain't they? The ones what do it now are no Einsteins, I know. From all walks of life and with no outstanding talent other than being able to get on with people and to have the gift of the gab, that's all. Chrissake! It don't take much brain power to do that now, does it? Anyway, some of the other blokes enrolled on this course are not bad geezers really. From all walks of life, one of them a fairly wealthy businessman by all accounts. Got this thing about wanting to appear on tely, like. Seems he's always wanted to. As I say, takes all sorts.

During the week, I have to travel back to me home-town to take part in a dress rehearsal for s the Cabaret Show that I'm involved in at the Wufton Town Hall. Turns out to be great fun, don't it? And it's all good experience for me, ain't it? Oh, I know it's only the pensioners who'll be watching, but it don't matter, does it? I feels it's a privilege to entertain them along with me other fellow artists, like. As I say, the actual rehearsal for the Show is actually in the Town Hall itself, so all of us in the cast has a chance to acclimatise ourselves with the place, don't we? Must say the acoustics of the Hall is bloody marvellous. We runs through the Show, and apart from one or two mistakes here and there, it don't go too bad. Rodney, the musical director, seems well pleased with it as far as he's concerned anyway. He has his full band of musicians present for the occasion, don't he? This consists of him on piano; Lisa, the RE teacher, on trombone; the PE geezer on French bleeding horn; David, the history man, on trumpet; and Brad, the maths teacher, on drums. So you can see we got quite a good back up for it all really. The producer of the Show, Dorothy, is having fifty fits all the while we're performing, ain't she? S'pose it's only natural really – them what's in charge always finding faults where another person wouldn't probably notice any. She's standing out in front of the stage observing our run through and chain-smoking herself to bleeding death, ain't she?

"I think we should have Mary making her entrance from the other side of the stage, don't you, Mr Randle?" she asks the headmaster of the school for his opinion, who, by the way, has come along and will be actually appearing in the Show doing a comedy act on the night, and who is now standing out front alongside her.

"I ag'wee," the old boy lisps. "I also think the film section people should sp'wead themselves out –too bunched up, Do'wothy."

"Mmm. Yes, I see what you mean."

So everyone sorts out what they gotta do on the night, don't they? Yours truly is performing in a couple of the sections, like. I even get to do me 'Double-Cross' number toward the end of the Show. Must admit that all the cast is a great bunch of guys and dolls really. The school's headmistress is also taking part, you know. Only trouble is the fact that she's busted her arm, like, and naturally, she looks a bit out of place up there on the stage with it all stuck in plaster. Did it iceskating, I believe. She's a game old bird though and is not letting this mishap interfere with her recitation of a well-known monologue that opens the second half of the Show, is she?

After rehearsals, I pops in the pub to see me parents before shooting off back to Simon's place at Harrow in me old jalopy-like, don't I?

"How's things with you then, Henry?" me old man asks after he's bought me a brown ale, and I'm sitting down at the table with the usual corner-of-the-bar crowd.

"Fine, thanks, Pa," I tells him, pleased to be in their company again. Seems such a long time since I was last here. Funny how you miss people, ain't it? Especially those of your family.

"Hear you're living with the snobs these days, Henry?" Stench remarks, sitting behind swigging beer.

"Y...e...a...h," Jason drawls, standing at the bar to the left.

"Heard any more about the TV talent show, Joey?" the landlord enquires, pulling a pint of the best.

"Oh, that reminds me, Henry," me ma says excitedly, fumbling in her handbag to fish out a letter for my attention. "This came for you this morning."

It's all quiet as I opens the letter. And sure enough, it's from the BBC, ain't it? I hurriedly reads its contents to meself.

"Y-e-s!" I cries out loud with excitement after digesting its contents. "They want me to appear on Chance of a Lifetime next Monday, don't they?"

"Gee! Henree," Jason heaves a contented sigh at hearing this news. "You sure as hell gonna appear on that little ol' telly after all then, buddy?"

"Well done! Henry – good luck to you, lad," the landlord congratulates me.

"Won't wanna speak with our sort afore long, I know," Stench remarks quietly, showing no signs of excitement like the others at me good fortune. "Turn you into a right toffee-nose they will, Henry – mark me words."

"Don't talk so bloody daft!" me old man explodes angrily at this remark from Stench. "Cos they bloody well won't. Don't know what you're ranting on about half the time, that's your trouble, silly old sod!"

"Well, I do hope you do well, Henry," the landlord adds, ringing up his cash register. "Must dash – Disco Night upstairs. Better check on things. Be seeing you then, Henry."

I bids Tom farewell as I finishes me drink. "Best be going meself I s'pose."

"You take care now," Ma implores with a worried frown.

"When will we see you again, lad?" Pa smiles proudly.

"I'll be down for the Show at the Town Hall Saturday. I've reserved you and Ma a couple of tickets. You are coming?"

"'Course we are. By the way, you make sure you have a word with Carol when you see her now?

"It's her big night Saturday, remember?" Ma reminds me. "So don't you go spoiling it for her now, Henry?"

"I hear she's Car...niv...al Queen this ye...ar, Henree," Jason remarks in his Clark Gable impersonation.

"That's right, Jason. And a fine one she will make, too," I assures him, real proud of this fact concerning Carol, like.

"Why don't you pop 'round and see her before journeying to Harrow, Henry?" me ma urges me to do so.

But as much as I'd like to, I don't think I will. She's probably out somewhere with lover boy Tarp anyway. "No, I'll be seeing her Saturday, won't I? Best be going then."

Everyone wishes me well for me BBC Show as I departs through the swing doors. As I do, a Salvation Army officer greets me with a smile on his way into the boozer, don't he? I drops a few coppers in the money box he's carrying before we departs company, a War Cry publication tucked under me arm as I makes in the direction of the Car Park. The Disco in the bar above is really jumpin' now, and the noise that's coming from the place is nobody's business, I can tell you. I gazes up prior to getting into me jalopy and notices the landlord and Basher, the bouncer, talking together out on the balcony. No doubt they're reckoning on how much profit the evening's entertainment is making for them? I have heard that Basher is taking himself off to the south of France on holiday once the gig is over. All right for some, ain't it? Bleeding south of France indeed! Jeez! I'll be lucky if I gets as far as Brighton this year, won't I? Either that, or else good old Southend, like. It won't be the same though without Carol wherever I go, will it? So I'm not particularly worried really. At the moment I just wanna see how things work out for me, like. I mean, I'm not even working for a living at present, am I? No doubt you must be wondering where I'm getting me money to live on, I bet. After all, I do have to contribute towards the rent at Simon's pad, don't I? But I'm okay, ain't I? Cos you see I collected me superannuation money when I left Tarp's employment, didn't I? There's also holiday pay into the bargain. So, all things considered, I'm managing quite well really. And once I get this modelling course behind me I can start earning some big money, can't I? Least, if what Simon says is true, I shall, that's for sure.

In all then I'm quite busy as you can see. And I'm well settled in up at Harrow now. Nice part of the world it is. Simon also has me running around various friends and acquaintances delivering them his fun packages, Seems a great demand for them.

"No harm in it sunshine!" he tells me one day. "Earns you a few bob, don't it? Just keep going to the places I tell you to and Fanny's your bleedin' aunt! Simple as that."

"But what if I ever get caught, Simon – what then?" I asks him with trepidation on this day in question.

"Look, Henry…" he begins explaining, "It's not as if you're handling the hard stuff – cos you ain't, see. Ever heard of art, sunshine? Well, that's what these pictures represent, don't they? The hoo…man body in its true natural beauty."

"Yeah – that maybe so. But some of those photos… Cor! Bit much, ain't they?"

Simon lights himself a cigar. "There ain't nothing wrong in making love, Henry. Better than making war any day, ain't it?

Dunno why people gets so heated up over a few simple pictures showing a man and a woman doing what comes naturally to 'em. Nothing at all wrong in that you know, ol' boy?"

I tell you – by the time Simon's finished lecturing he has me convinced that some of these pictures I'm hawking about is indeed works of bleeding art. Must admit, the old sod does have a certain charm about him. I reckon he'd get away with murder if he had to.

Anyway, this courier game is handy as a sideline for me till I gets sorted out with a full time position, like. Pays the rent, don't it? So, in all I'm quite excited about everything. There's the Show at the Town Hall on Saturday, then Chance of a Lifetime at the BBC on Monday.

With me present working timetable I gets plenty of time to rehearse for them both, don't I? I'm somewhat uncertain as to how this telly thing will go cos it says in the letter that three of us artists are to appear in the package, Simon, like me, being included in this number. May the best man bleeding well win, eh?

"Funny that they should pick us two for the Show, ain't it, Henry?" Simon says to me after I arrives back home from rehearsals.

"Yeah…" is all I can think of to say to this question. I only hope our friendship continues once the thing's all over if one of us just happens to win it, like? I mean, there's people fall out over less, ain't there?

"Heh! Hear the one about the toilet attendant who keeps complaining about the cold inside his loo?" Simon tries a joke out on me. Seems he's having an early night for a change. He's gotta be up early in the morning to film a TV commercial, ain't he? "Well, his mate tells him to install a paraffin heater inside the place to keep it warm, don't he? 'Wot!' the toilet attendant says to him, "an' stink the bloody place out – you must be jokin'!"

I can't help laughing, can I? Simon's jokes are a right giggle, ain't they? I've heard worse, I can tell you. I reckon he'll go down a bomb on the Big Chance, I really do. Then again, you don't know what they're really looking for, do you? It's all down to the general viewer in the end though I suppose. As the saying goes – they either like you or they don't. Just have to wait and see, don't we?

"Wonder how things will go for us on Monday, Henry?" Simon asks when we're lying in our beds staring up at the ceiling later.

"Yeah – I wonder?" I says, starting to feel quite excited about the whole business now.

"No hard feelings if one of us manages to get through, eh, sunshine?"

"No – course not."

Simon stubs his cigar out in the ashtray by his bedside. "Rehearsals go all right tonight, Henry?"

"Fine, thanks. Should go well Saturday. Mayor of Wufton'll be there on the night. Also Reggie Summers – the TV geezer, you know?"

And so will my Carol, I thinks, smiling to meself at the thought. Be nice seeing her again, I must say.

Simon turns on his side to face me. "You don't have to deliver any more of my packages if you don't want to you, Henry," he says to me quietly.

I peers across at him in the darkened room. I can hear the electric trains in the distance pulling in and out the station. "It's okay, Simon," I replies. "I don't mind – honest."

"You sure?"

"Yeah – I'm sure."

What's this – Simon getting a guilty conscience? After all, it is me rent money we're talking about here, ain't it? But then a terrible thought occurs to me. What if I don't make good in this here modelling game. What then? And also what if this Big Chance programme doesn't come to anything? Negative thinking, I know; but then it means I'll be relying solely on these porn bleeding packages to earn a crust, don't it? Least – till I gets fixed up with something else anyway.

I turns over to face the wall, mumbling quietly to meself.

"What's that, sunshine?"

"Oh, nothing – negative thoughts, that's all."

Simon tries cheering me up. "What say we have a day out at the Lido on Sunday, Henry?"

"Sounds a good idea. Yeah – why not? "Right – count me in."

"Do us both good to get away and forget about things."

"Okay."

And with this pleasant thought in mind we both soon drops off to sleep, don't we?

Chapter 7

So Saturday duly arrives, don't it? And finds me travelling to Wufton behind the wheel of me old banger in the direction of the Town Hall for this here senior citizens concert. Me guitar's lying on the back seat, and I'm feeling pretty happy with life and with things in general. I'm wearing casual gear with a colourful bead necklace that I bought from a trinket shop up in Harrow before leaving. The car radio's playing pop music to accompany me on my journey, so I'm keeping the beat by tapping me foot on the floorboard, being careful not to get too carried away in case I manage to put it through the floorboard, like. Who knows – they may even play one of my records soon if I'm lucky enough to break into the music business? Be a right laugh that would, cos then I'd show 'em what our Henry's made of, wouldn't I? 'Specially Tarp. I s'pose he'll be along tonight during the interval to gape at Carol while she's being crowned Carnival Queen? Don't suppose she'll find time to talk with me, will she? Cos I know for a fact that he's taking her out on the town once the ceremony's completed, ain't he? Ah, well… good luck to her is all I can say really. After all, she is a nice gal, that's for sure.

Me and my beloved old jalopy disappears into the jaws of the concrete canyon on arriving at Wufton, the Town Hall clearly in sight as I emerges safely on the other side. I then head for the car park at the rear of this building.

"Henry! Hello!"

It's Dorothy, the producer. She's standing by her car, her arms laden with numerous dresses and other items needed for the Show. She's all dolled up, and is wearing a long, blue evening dress for the special occasion. Her husband, Peter, who, by the way, is props manager for our Association, is trying with a certain amount of difficulty to lock their car door owing to him also having his arms full.

"How's it going, Henry?" he greets me jovially, despite his predicament with the car keys. I've always found him to be a jolly sorta chap at heart.

"Mustn't grumble," I tells him, grabbing me guitar from the back seat of the car.

"Here! Hold this will you, mate?" He hands me a case for safekeeping.

"What on earth's in here – it weighs a ton?"

"That, Henry…" Dorothy proceeds to explain, still managing to puff away at a cigarette she's somehow got wedged between her fingers beneath all the garb she's carrying, "is what might be termed as our emergency survival kit!"

"Your what!"

"Our emergency survival kit!" Peter repeats with a certain amount of pride.

"I see," I says, but I bleeding well don't really. I haven't a clue what the hell he's on about, have I? All is revealed, however, as Peter then opens their box of tricks, like. And what do you think is inside? You'd never guess. Bottles of whisky and gin, ain't there? I ask you? Unbelievable.

"See what we mean, Henry?"

In the meantime the school bus rolls into the car park, heavily laden with the larger stage props. The driver of this vehicle is a young, fair-haired bloke who is the religious teacher at the school, like. He pulls to a stop and jumps down.

"Hi everyone!" he squeaks in a high pitched voice. This fella's not a bad singer as it happens. His rendition of *Donkey Serenade* is quite something with his large straw sombrero hat perched askew on top of his head. A donkey on stage for him to sit astride would have been the ultimate in authenticity.

"Managed to get everything on board then, Alan?" Dorothy enquires.

"Yes – just about, I think," he chirps excitedly.

"Give you a hand to unload in a minute," Peter assures him. "Just want to check the stage lights first."

So we heads off in the direction of the artists entrance round the back of the Hall, don't we? It's not long afterwards that the rest of the cast and backstage hands all arrives and we commence to get ourselves ready for the Show. Seems there's to be an interval half way through, in which time the Carnival Queen is crowned by the TV geezer, Reggie Summers.

As time draws near to start, we're told by the headmaster of the school that the Hall's packed out with pensioners what's arrived in numerous coaches to see us. It's the headmaster who will actually be putting everyone out front in the picture soon when he and Dorothy sit on stage throughout the performance giving a bit of chat, like, and explaining to the audience what's going on. He even plays the part of a villain in a short Victorian melodrama that follows shortly after the interval. Yeah – he's a real right one, ain't he? Not many blokes in his position would do the same, I'm thinking.

The Show eventually gets under way as we hear the introductory music being played by the Band, giving us all our cue to move on stage to sing our opening number. We're all feeling bleeding nervous, I can tell you. It goes down quite well though, despite one or two of us forgetting our words; but I don't think anyone really notices, for we receive a big round of applause as we finish, don't we?

Backstage, it's all excitement as various artists prepare themselves before going on to perform their acts, like. There's one or two panic stations though, as some of us have quick changes to do before dashing back on stage. As I say, the Show is called Cabaret and the stage is set like a nightclub, with bottles of wine and everything arranged so as to create the atmosphere of an actual cabaret show. Know what I mean? The affect is quite something really.

Anyway, we gets through the first half, like, and it seems to be a success. During the interval our producer calls us all together and says, "Could I have your attention, please...! Thank you. To those of you who are thinking of going across the road to the pub for a drink... well, would you please be back here ready to start the second half in twenty minutes... Okay? Twenty minutes!"

A few moans greet this message as a sudden stampede makes for the door and down the stairs by those who wanna partake in a drink, which is just about everybody really, ain't it? All, that is, apart from me, Dorothy and her husband and the headmaster. My reason for staying is pretty obvious. I'm gonna watch Carol get crowned Carnival Queen, ain't I? The others are stopping because they've got their own drinks with Peter's survival kit, ain't they? So I leaves them guzzling and goes down to witness the crowning ceremony.

Up till now I ain't even laid eyes on Carol, have I? I heard someone mention that she'd arrived while I was on stage with two other blokes performing 'I'm Getting Married in the Morning'; but as I say, I don't actually see her, do I? Not until this precise moment, that is, as I catches sight of her as I comes through into the Hall. She's up on stage with two delightful lady escorts to chaperone her as she sits in her chair with a mauve cape draped around her, underneath which she's wearing this immaculate long, white evening dress. And she looks positively marvellous, don't she? Takes me breath away just looking at her. She's just this minute been crowned Queen and has this sparkling crown perched on top of her lovely fair-haired head. This geezer Reggie Summers is standing speaking with her, while the local Gazette photographer is popping flash bulbs all over the place taking pictures of her, ain't he?

Then the TV guy addresses the audience: "Could we have a big hand... a large round of applause, please, ladies and gentlemen! For this year's local Carnival Queen, your very own, Miss Carol Shelley!"

And while everyone is giving Carol a nice big hand, our Reggie Summers plants a kiss on her lips before making his exit from the scene. No doubt he's charged a bloody fortune for his few minutes' effort, ain't he? Still, I s'pose if you can get away with it, why the hell not, eh?

Then it's the mayor's turn to come up on stage. He gives a short speech about how pleased he is to see so many of the senior citizens of the town all gathered together on this, their annual night out.

"But we mustn't forget the efforts of Lancing School though, must we?" he continues, glancing at some notes in his hand. "After all, I think they are putting on a real great show for us tonight, wouldn't you agree?"

More applause. It's nice to know we're appreciated, ain't it?

"All that remains for me to do now is to kiss our lovely Carnival Queen for this year and to tell you to make your way out into the small Hall where, I believe, there are some light refreshments waiting for you. So thank you very much, ladies and gentlemen! Goodnight! And may God bless you all!"

The old mayor walks over to Carol and kisses her on the cheek, don't he? I'm tempted to do the same meself; but I'll have to wait, won't I?

While most of the people present are taking refreshments, I takes the opportunity to go over the other side of the stage to where Carol is now making her way down the steps. Its then that I bumps into old Tarp, ain't it?

"Good evening, Higgins!" he addresses me. He's all done up like a dog's dinner in a bleeding monkey suit, ain't he? The lot – dickybow tie, everything.

"Watcha!" I greets him. No bleeding airs and graces with me, mate, I can tell you.

"A very good Show if I may say so," he compliments the school's association on the evening's entertainment they've so far provided.

"I'm glad you're enjoying it."

"Quite the entertainer, aren't we, Higgins?"

"I enjoy it."

Carol then joins our company, don't she? God! She really does take me breath away, what with her beautiful dress and everything.

"Hello! Henry," she greets me with her lovely smile. "How have you been keeping then?"

"I'm fine, thanks Carol," I gulps, feeling all funny inside, see, as I stands there just looking at her. She really looks gorgeous, with her blue eyes sparkling with excitement. I don't think I've ever seen her looking so attractive in me life before. No wonder she won the bleeding beauty contest. With her around, none of the other gals stood a chance, did they?

"How's the Show going – sung your song yet, have you?" she enquires sweetly.

"Not yet, no," I informs her.

And that's where our conversation comes to an abrupt end, don't it? Cos old Tarp butts in, don't he?

"Pity we can't stay and watch you perform, Higgins," he says all bleeding maliciously, like. "You see – I shall be taking Carol out to dinner and a cabaret show all of our own."

Is that bloody so? I thinks to meself as I stands gazing into Carol's eyes. I can see she is embarrassed by what the silly old sod's just said, like. Showing me up is all he's trying do, ain't he? The creep.

"I really do think we should be going, my dear," he addresses Carol. My dear, indeed. Huh! Makes you sick, dunnit?

But Carol, bless her little heart, stands her ground, don't she? "Would you mind if I just spend a minute or two with Henry, Charles?" she almost pleads for this request. So its Charles now, too, is it? Talk about the bleeding brush off, mate!

"Very well – but do hurry or we'll be late. I'll wait outside in the car for you."

So Tarp makes his exit, leaving me and Carol alone together for a moment. I can see she's finding it hard to talk as she fumbles with the bouquet of flowers she's holding.

"What you wanna say, Carol?" I finally asks her.

"Just that I'm… well, sorry, Henry," she manages to blurt out tearfully.

"For what, luv?"

"Well… for running out on your Show in this way."

I pretends I don't mind. "S'all right – can't be helped. 'Specially as you and Tarp have ordered your candlelit dinner together."

From over in the refreshment Hall the noise of cups and saucers rattling and of people chatting can be heard.

"Does my going with Charles make you jealous then, Henry?"

To say I bleeding well ain't would only be telling a lie, wouldn't it? "Thought you said there was nothing going on between you?" I questions Carol on this sore subject – at least as far as I'm concerned, it is.

She hesitates for a moment, before answering: "I also seem to remember you saying that you weren't interested in me anymore, Henry?"

"Never said anything of the sort, gal," I says in defence of this accusation. "All I said was that I weren't interested in getting married yet. And I'm still not, see?"

"All right, all right – I best be going if we're going to argue about it."

Carol's perfectly right, of course. 'Specially as it's such a big occasion for her, like. "I'm – I'm sorry, luv," I says to her softly. "Shouldn't go upsetting you tonight of all nights, should I?"

She glances down at her pretty bunch of flowers. "It's okay, Henry – I understand."

But I can see that it ain't really. There's something on the gal's mind, that's for sure. "Come on, Carol – what do you really wanna say to me?"

She looks deep into my eyes, searching, it seems, for something – for what though?

"What I really wanted to know was whether you still felt the same about settling down and everything?" she enquires of me tentatively.

"And judging by what you say, I can obviously see that you do, Henry."

"And you must have a good reason for asking me, Carol?" I puts to her forcibly.

Then I twigs it, don't I? Bleeding Tarp's got designs on marrying her himself, ain't he, I bet? And judging by the look Carol's now giving me, I can see that she knows what I'm thinking, too. So that's their bloody game, is it? Well, call me a monkey's uncle! Who'd have thought it?

"Yes, Henry – Charles wants to marry me," she calmly informs me, having obviously read my mind on the subject.

Even so, this news hits me hard, don't it? Sledgehammer job, ain't it? Know what I mean? "You – you can't be serious, luv?"

"It's true, yes."

"But – but when, for Chrissake?"

71

"There's – there's something of importance I think you should know first though, Henry?"

But before Carol has a chance to explain what this something is, old bloody Tarp's standing by her side again, ain't he?

"We really must be going, my dear," he addresses her, dragging her away from me.

Then they're gone, ain't they? Leaving me standing there like a right bloody lemon, not knowing what she was about to relate to me. Still, if it's that important, she can get in touch, can't she?

The next thing I know is I'm being told it's time for the second half of the Show to commence. It goes down pretty well; but I don't really enjoy it much cos of what Carol's told me about her and Tarp. I mean – the geezer's twice her age, ain't he? In fact, old enough to be her father. Surely she won't marry him? Stranger things do happen though I s'pose – and if that's what she really wants, then it's none of my damn business, is it?

So – as the old saying goes – the Show must go on, mustn't it? There's somewhat of a hold up in getting things under way after the interval as it happens. Seems the Band is missing on parade, ain't they? All of them, it appears, except for the musical director, is still over at the pub putting the pints away. Cos, Rodney's doing his little nut, ain't he?

"Disgraceful behaviour!" he fumes, pacing up and down the corridor waiting for his musicians to appear on the scene. "Surely they know it's time for them to be back now?"

And to make matters worse, once the Show does eventually restart, one of the musicians pours a bottle of light ale into the mouth of Lisa's trombone, so that when she starts playing, it sprays just about everyone within five yards radius of the bloody instrument with beer, don't it? Laugh! Poor old Lisa – the look on her face – you should have seen it. But she seems to take it all in good spirit. As I've told you, I don't enjoy participating so much this half, do I?

Everything goes well though, with some good performances coming from young Ned, a coloured guy who sings *Ol Man River*. Nice voice – deep bass. And then there's Taffy, a Welsh tenor who sings *Welcome in the Hillside* for us, which is always a good song to get the audience going with. *Donkey Serenade* goes down well, too – Alan singing his heart out with this particular number. Yours truly doesn't do bad neither with me 'Double-Cross' number, do I? Then Dorothy herself gives her rendition of *Burlington Bertie*, which proves to be very popular with everyone, especially the mayor, who's on his feet cheering at the end of it.

With the conclusion of the finale we all receive a generous round of applause for our efforts, particularly our musical director, despite the beer-spraying fanfare at the opening of the second half. Then our producer, Dorothy, is presented with a lovely bouquet of flowers for her efforts, ain't she? So just about everyone is well pleased at the way it's turned out; but above all, the pensioners themselves seemed to have thoroughly enjoyed the evening's entertainment, don't they? Which is the most important aspect of all.

On my return journey to Harrow later that evening, I must admit I did feel a little sad. Sad that the Show had to end, and mostly cos of Carol having decided to settle down with old Tarp in matrimony. I mean – it'll never last, will it? Stands to reason. She's bound to eventually tire of him, ain't she? There's no go in the man, miserable old sod. Maybe it's sour grapes on my part I s'pose. I reckon though that Carol must have a pretty good reason if she does go ahead and marry the geezer.

Simon's not in when I arrives back at the flat, is he? So I goes straight to bed, don't I? I'm feeling pretty exhausted, I can tell you. Do me good to have an early night anyway. Tomorrow, we have this day out at the Lido that Simon's arranged, so that will take me mind off things, won't it? Knowing Simon, there's bound to be some gals present to make me forget about Carol though.

As I turn in for the night and about to switch off the bedside lamp, I suddenly remembers I've forgotten to check to see if me parents were at the Show tonight. Fancy that?

Chapter 8

And what do you think? The very next morning – bright and early, like, I'm awakened from my slumber by a lovely looking dolly who's made me a cuppa tea and whose name, I'm soon to learn is Bobbie. Wanna see her, she's quite something, with auburn hair and wearing one of Simon's towel dressing gowns.

"Well, hello there, Henry!" she greets me, after placing the tea on the bedside table for my convenience. "I'm a friend of Simon's – in case you're wondering?"

I sits up in bed, rubbing me eyes to make sure this beauty before me is not a figment of me imagination, like. The curtains in the room have been drawn and the sunlight from outside is streaming in, heralding a fine day. Just right for our planned trip.

"A friend of Simon's, eh?" I questions this bubbly bundle of joy perched next to me on the bed.

"Yes – that's right," she replies with a friendly smile.

She really is a humdinger, with tantalising green eyes and a pair of scrumptious boobs protruding through the top of Simon's dressing gown like nobody's business, ain't they?

I sips me tea and pretends not to notice. Who am I kidding though? "Simon around anywhere?" I questions this illustrious beauty that's entered my life.

"He's gone on ahead – with Michelle." She pouts her lips sexily. "Told me to fetch you along later if that's all right with you?"

"Sure thing," I says in full agreement with this suggestion. Be a bloody fool not to, wouldn't I?

Bobbie then fills me in with what's been happening, like. Seems the three of them – Simon, Bobbie and this gal called Michelle arrives back here in the early hours of the morning from a party. Michelle shacks up with lucky Simon, while this Bobbie beauty sleeps on the sofa, don't she? In the other room, of course. All above board, know what I mean?

"Comfy, was it – the sofa?" I enquires with a slightly guilty conscience knowing that I have had the best of the deal where sleeping arrangements were concerned last night. But then, I wasn't to know, was I – about Bobbie, I mean?

"Wasn't too bad – have slept on worse", Bobbie assures me, lighting a cigarette and offering me one at the same time. "Do you use them?"

"No, not one of me vices, thanks, luv."

She gives me the once over with her seductive green eyes. She really does look sexy. "You do have some vices, don't you, Henry?"

I don't answer, cos I'm not quite sure how to answer this particular question, am I? After all, I s'pose everyone has some vice or other, don't they? So I finishes me tea, and am about to jump out of bed when I realises I'm wearing no pyjamas, am I? I dunno – right carry on, ain't it?

"Could you pass me my dressing gown, please, Bobbie?"

Her eyes seem to light up at my request, and I notices her staring at me manly chest. Well… I do have a few hairs growing there, don't I?

"Sleep in the raw, do you, darling?" Bobbie comments with a mischievous smile upon her face, passing me the gown from the foot of the bed.

"The only way this weather."

"I couldn't agree with you more."

After covering myself and rising from the bed, I ask her: "You're friends with Simon, you say?"

"Yes." She stubs her cigarette out in the ashtray, and gets to her feet. "We'll get ready, shall we, and join them?"

I notices how tall she is. Wanna see her – six feet at least, with green-painted toenails. Kinky, eh! "Yes – let's," I agrees with her suggestion.

Bobbie then glides over to be closer to me, my old ticker going ten to the dozen, like. Is she about to seduce me? I wonder. But me luck ain't in, is it? As she politely offers me her warm hand to shake. "I do hope we can be good friends, Henry?"

I goes along with these sentiments exactly, even though deep down I'm wishing the relationship between us could possibly be a little bit more than just platonic. But there you go – can't have everything, can we?

Fifteen minutes later we're driving fast along the road toward the Lido in Bobbie's sleek, red sports job, ain't we?

"Nice car" I comments, the sun shining down on us from a cloudless blue sky above and with a cool breeze ruffling our hair. My delightful companion is dressed in blue denim jacket and slacks, and with make-up on she looks even more attractive than back at the flat.

"I like it," she answers, the red head scarf she's wearing fluttering in the breeze. She seems a very competent driver, I must say.

"Work in London, do you, Bobbie?" I'm eager to become better acquainted with this auburn-haired beauty seated beside me on this wonderful summer day.

We journey down the hill, passing the church spire that's showing prominently high above the green cluster of trees away to our left, a well-known landmark of Harrow, at the rear of which the renowned Harrow school is actually situated. You know – the one where all those toffee-nosed perishers privileged enough to be educated go? I dunno – all right for some, ain't it?

"Sometimes London, perhaps Paris. America occasionally, if I'm lucky," Bobbie replies to the question. "Depends what the agency finds for us."

I glances across at her. "I see," I says, but I don't really, do I? S'pose I should start finding out about these things seeing as I might be lucky enough to secure work in some of these famous places? You can never tell? After all, once I've completed me training at this here Charm School I'm attending, I just might? There's also the BBC. Who knows where that may lead? U S of A maybe? Perhaps my 'Double-Cross' song'll climb straight to the top of the hit parade? These possibilities are open to me really now, ain't they? Just need the right break, that's all. And a bit of luck as well.

"Simon says you might be entering the modelling profession yourself, Henry?"

"Could well be," I replies; but I don't sound all that confident. Which is only natural I s'pose – considering how she's in the same game, like. No good me trying to pull the wool over this gal's eyes with bullshit about the line of business she's making a living from now, is there? Soon tumble me, wouldn't she? Wise to all the tricks of the trade, I should think.

Bobbie swings her car round a sharp bend in the road, changing expertly down the gears as she does so. Confidence just seems to ooze from this gal. Maybe some might rub off on me? I sincerely hope so.

"I think you'll do all right at modelling," Bobbie smiles, taking her eyes off the road for a moment to glance at me. "Confidence is all it needs. And bloody hard work, of course?"

"Of course."

"You'll be just fine, Henry – you'll see."

"I hope so," I sighs despondently.

"My, my, but we are feeling down, aren't we?" Bobbie's hand suddenly strays from the gear stick to rest in me lap, don't it?

I pretends not to notice her green-fingered hand rubbing the inside of me thigh as I starts getting all hot under the collar, like. Know what I mean?

"I believe you and Simon have a similar kind of background, don't you – working class?"

"Is that a bad thing then in your game?"

Her warm hand moves forward to grip the gear lever once again. Much to my regret, of course. I mean, fancy being seduced in an open top sports job with a chick like Bobbie? Now that would be something. But there's a time and a place for everything, ain't there?

"It's neither good nor bad as I see it, Henry. Doesn't really matter where you're from. One's upbringing should make no difference. I know I was extremely lucky – born into fairly upper class, you know? True – it has its advantages – education and everything. I was privileged to attend Cheltenham School for girls, Henry."

"Well, jolly bloody hockey sticks to you then, gal!" I cracks with a laugh. Couldn't resist it, could I? "Secondary Mod, me, you know?"

Bobbie's hand wanders to find me soft spot again, like. Crazy! Seems all I have to do is seek a little sympathy, and I gets this treatment, don't I? Great, ain't it?

"Doesn't worry me, Henry, you not being an academic."

"An acawot?"

"A scholar, darling!"

And judging by the way she's fondling me down there, it's certainly the truth she's speaking, ain't it? I mean, it's usually us fellas what has to make the first move. Still, why shouldn't the ladies show a bit of initiative where sex is concerned for a change? Let them get their faces slapped instead, eh? Talk about laugh.

She removes her hand just as I'm about to burst a blood vessel. "You and Simon seem to have hit it off together from what I've been told?"

"Yeah – you could say that," I agrees with her statement, which, I s'pose is true cos we do, don't we?

"Probably because you are so much alike," Bobbie adds.

"Are we?" I'm sitting back enjoying the ride, the breeze cooling down this sexual urge that she's managed to arouse in me.

"Oh, very much so," she states. "Both creative types, aren't you? I hear you are to appear together on television?"

"Yeah – Chance of a Lifetime for the BBC...Next week, matter a fact. Never know – could mean a break for a lucky someone?"

"Sounds exciting. Singer, aren't you?"

"Play guitar as well. Also write me own songs. Doing one Monday, I've called it *Double-Cross Baby*.

"Really? That's wonderful."

By now we're arriving at the Lido, ain't we? Where Bobbie finds a parking space before we walks on down to the entrance together.

"Got your costume with you?" I ask my charming companion after we've paid and squeezed through the turnstiles.

"Mine is in town, I'm afraid. Doesn't matter – I'll swim nude!"

For a moment I think the gal is serious, don't I? But I notice her smiling, and I realise she's only fooling around. "I wonder where Simon and Michelle are?" she enquires, gazing about the crowded grass enclosure in front of the bathing area. The gorgeous weather's obviously brought everyone out for the afternoon.

"Search me," I replies, me eyes almost popping out their sockets at seeing so many lovelies stretched out on the grass in their swim wear in front of the expanse of water that's glistening in the brightness beyond.

"They could be anywhere." Bobbie is weaving her way through the cluster of bodies, being careful not to step on anyone. "Perhaps they're swimming?"

We find a vacant spot beneath the shade of an old oak tree and decide to settle there.

"Never mind – they'll find us soon. Phew! It's certainly hot, isn't it?"

At this, Bobbie immediately peels off her clothes and lays down on her back in the sun that's filtering through the leaves of the tree above. She's wearing just her panties and bra, and you wanna know something? She looks just about the sexiest gal at the Lido, don't she? Mind – she's displaying this superb suntan to add to her beauty, like, ain't she? Probably obtained from a South-of France holiday sometime recently. Maybe she may have rubbed shoulders with our old friend Basher from the pub while she was there? I dunno – crazy old world we live in, ain't it?

I, too, slips me clothes off. Mind – I do have me swimming trunks on underneath, don't I? Unlike my partner though, I have no suntan to display, and me skin is sickly-white in comparison.

As I mentioned, there's plenty of people around…Kiddies screeching and playing in the water, while at intervals water skiers swoosh by the bank behind a speedboat. Music also fills the air from tranny radios with DJ's keeping us up to date with the latest pop hits. "And now, folks! We have none other than the latest young singer to hit the scene – Henry Higgins! With this weeks' number one spot…! Wait for it…! Yes, you've guessed! Double-Cross Baby…!"

Hah! Be a right laugh, that would, wouldn't it? Still – never know. Could happen. Gotta keep telling meself this anyway, ain't I?

But seriously, I quite like it here at the Lido. Nice area – clean, respectable. Know what I mean? Wouldn't mind settling down here someday. You know – maybe marriage? Perhaps purchase a small house nearby? Could pop to the Lido often as I fancy then, couldn't I? My thoughts suddenly turn to Carol, don't they? And I wonder what she might be doing now, and if she's still contemplating marrying old Tarp? I don't think she will, mind. But you never know – dames are funny where marriage is concerned, ain't they?

"Uhmm…" I sighs, sitting up, my eyes taking in the beauty of Bobbie as she lays stretched out on the grass beside me. Wanna see her. She's even wearing green panties and bra, ain't she? Bloody hell! I mean, any bloke would be tempted, wouldn't they?

"Don't you care?" I question her on the state of her flimsy attire. "I mean – just lying there in your underwear?"

She don't even so much as raise an eyelid, does she? "Mind?" she purrs quietly, swatting a fly that's come to rest on her very sensual belly button. "Why should I mind?"

"Well… what people might say – think? "

She lifts her curved body slowly from the grass, turning onto her side to rest on her elbow. She looks up at me, her lovely green eyes squinting in the bright sunlight. "There are girls here today who are wearing even less than I am with their flimsy bikinis. You don't mind them, do you, Henry? So why all the fuss about me lying in the sun in my perfectly respectful undergarments? No bloody harm in it, is there?"

What could I say? Obviously, Bobbie feels perfectly at home in what she's doing, don't she? "No – s'pose not," I answers her question finally.

"I mean… you're actually showing more of your body than I am, darling."

She's absolutely right, of course. "Fair comment; but let's not quarrel over it, eh?"

She snuggles up close to me. "I'm not arguing, Henry – just stating a fact." She pauses to examine my body in more detail. "I mean… you have rather a nice body. Everybody has a nice body, come to think of it really, don't they?"

"Let's not carried away now, gal."

But I can see Bobbie is not one to be put off, is she? For suddenly her soft hand is caressing my inside leg again. Jeez! Not here, surely. Not that I mind. Bleeding hell! Who would? But right here on the grass in the middle of the Lido? Not on, is it? I mean – what if a bloke has to stand up suddenly or something? Stick out a mile, wouldn't he?

"So?" Bobbie persists in running her fingers up and down me leg. What's she trying to do – play a tune or something? Mozart's flute concerto – get what I mean? Bloody laugh though, ain't it? "… Why are we ashamed of our bodies, Henry?"

Before I has chance to offer an explanation, which I haven't got anyway, there's voices calling both our names. "Heh! Henry…! Over here…!"

"Yoo – ooo…! Over here, Bobbie…!"

Bobbie is first to spot them. "There they are, look, Henry! Simon and Michelle – see them?" She points in the direction of the Crazy Putting Green behind.

I recognises Simon who's shouting and waving a golf club around in the air excitedly. "Come over and join us, Henry…!"

Bobbie jumps to her feet to slip her clothes back on. "Come on, Henry – you'll be all right as you are", she says, racing over to be with them.

I decides to pull me shirt and trousers on first.

"Watcha, Henry!" Simon greets me cheerfully, an attractive looking gal hanging from his arm "Managed to get out of bed all right then?"

"So this is your roommate?" his blonde-haired beauty enquires, smiling.

"Yeah, that's him all right. Henry – I'd like you to meet Michelle, a modellin' friend of mine. Michelle, this is Henry, me ol' mucker."

We both shakes hands, and I notice she's not very tall, unlike Bobbie, who towers above all of us. She's also a little on the plump side, unusual, I would have thought, being in her profession. She certainly is attractive, with radiant, piercing blue eyes. Gorgeous figure that has a pretty pink, low cut summer dress clinging to it.

"Hi! Henry," she greets me with a warm, friendly smile… "Hope we didn't wake you last night?"

"Didn't hear a murmur?" I tell her truthfully.

"Dead to the world when he's in the land of nod – our Henry, I can tell you." Simon says.

"May we join you in your golf game, Simon?" Bobbie requests sweetly.

"Please – be our guests. You'll need some clubs though."

"I'll get them," I says, heading off in the direction of the deck-chair hut.

So we all play this game of crazy golf, don't we? It proves to be great fun and a laugh. Besides which there is the added attraction for me and Simon each time Michelle stoops to retrieve her little white ball. Wow! Some boobs, I tell you. I mean – no bra – nothing!

"This is the life, eh, Henry?" Simon comments, putting his ball down one of the holes. "Yes! Wonderful shot! Lee Travino eat your heart out!"

After the game, we returns to the spot where meself and Bobbie were earlier. Simon and Michelle opens up their tuck box and we all get stuck in to chicken legs, a variety of sandwiches and some chocolate cake. It leaves me agreeing with Simon's statement, don't it? Yes, this is indeed the life all right.

"Got your song all rehearsed for tomorrow, Henry?" he then asks, lying on his back, his head resting comfortably in Michelle's lap while he swigs beer from the ale bottle. Simon, by the way, is wearing a very snazzy white suit and sneakers to match for the occasion. Looks a right toff, don't he?

"I think so – yeah," I tells him, enjoying me cake. "You got everything sorted, have you?"

"Sure thing, sunshine. Slay 'em, I will – wait and see."

"Which of you will win, do you think?" Michelle asks, sipping her sherry.

"My money's definitely on Henry," Bobbie informs every one of her choice.

"You better watch her, Henry – has her eyes set on you, I think?" Michelle adds.

"I'm sure we'll behave like perfect gentlemen which ever one is successful, won't we sunshine?" Simon says with a wry grin on his face.

It's at this point of our conversation that I notices the particular tie he's wearing. Never seen one like it before. So, being the inquisitive type, I enquires politely: "Strange looking tie you have on, mate?"

Simon fingers the object in question as he examines it for a second or so. "Mean to say you haven't managed to acquire one of these yet, sunshine?"

The two gals start to snigger, don't they?

"Why? Should I have then?"

The gals continue their giggling.

"That depends, don't it?" Simon says, winking at them.

"On what?" I enquires, wondering what the hell everyone's finding so amusing.

"On whether or not you've had the operation, darling?" Michelle chuckles.

"Operation? What operation?"

"Vasectomy – only takes a few minutes. Just shows what the medical profession can do these days, don't it?"

The penny finally drops. "Chrissake!" I gasps with shock. "Surely you've not had that performed on you?"

"And why the hell not, may I ask?" Simon retaliates testily.

"Cos – that's why. I mean – what if you ever decides to settle down and get married – you won't be able to have any kids, will you? Crazy idea."

"Perhaps he doesn't want any more kids, Henry," Michelle tells me seriously.

"What on earth do you mean – more?"

"Didn't you know? Simon already has a child," Bobbie informs me.

"Oh…!" I says, flabbergasted at hearing this news.

Simon gets to his feet. "S'right, sunshine! Marriage went wrong, see. Nothing to be proud of. He's three years old now, the kid."

"Is he?"

"So I don't want to go in for any more. Nor marriage, neither. No thank you. Sorry – but that's the way I feel, me ol' china."

He obviously does feel upset about the whole business, don't he? Bit bloody drastic though, ain't it? Final, like? And to think they're handing out ties to encourage geezers to go in for the idea as well. I dunno – crazy old world we live in, that's for sure.

"Come on – let's go for a swim!" Simon suggests, changing the subject.

"Bobbie has no costume," I says.

"Don't worry about me, lads – I'll go in as I am – jeans and all!"

"Come on! Last one in's a cissy!"

So we hurriedly change into our bathing trunks and race along the embankment toward the swimming area. The place is packed, ain't it?

"Come on, you lot!" we can hear Bobbie calling us from somewhere in the water; but we don't see her cos there's so many other bathers, like.

"Over here!"

"There she is!" I cries, spotting her close to the raft-type platform in the water that's situated about fifty yards or so out.

So we all wades in at the shallow end and starts swimming out to this raft, which, by the way, is as far as anyone's allowed to venture cos of the water skiers using the area just beyond it. As I says, there's bodies everywhere thrashing about in the water.

"Nice and warm, ain't it?" Simon says when we've pulled ourselves up on the platform to join Bobbie. She's now lying stretched out on the raft, her clothes all dripping wet. She has swam across in them as she said she would, see. Looks a right sight, don't she?

It's Michelle whose last to make it over to us. She's not a very strong swimmer by the looks; but she finally grabs hold of the platform by Simon's feet where we're both sitting there dangling our feet in the water.

"Can you give a poor girl a hand up?" Michelle pleads, clutching at Simon's ankles.

But Simon only pushes her head under the water with his foot. "Get away with you," he jokes.

Michelle emerges again, gasping for air as she does so, like. "You devil…! You just wait!" she cries, clutching his foot, this time giving it a pull to send him toppling head first into the water alongside her. She goes into hysterics over this, pointing at Simon who's splashing about like a good 'un. "You should see the look on your face!"

"You little bastard!" Simon explodes, ducking her head under again.

"What on earth are you lot up to in there?" Bobbie asks, rising from her relaxed position on the raft to gander at these noisy proceedings. I gets to me feet, and prepares for a dive. "Race you to the other side, Bobbie!" I challenges me partner.

"Ughh…!" Simon gargles in the water below us. "Last one over pays for the first round of drinks tonight!"

So we all makes a bee-line for the other side, don't we? I'm not one to brag, like, but I know I'm a pretty good swimmer, and so I reaches our picnicking spot by the tree first. Simon's next, then Bobbie, and last of all is poor Michelle, who, by the time she drags herself from the water is pretty well near exhaustion, I can tell you.

"It's not fair!" she gasps, dropping onto the grass next to Simon.

"You're all better swimmers than me. It's just not fair!"

Simon rolls playfully on top of her, kissing her as he does so. "Never mind, my angel – won't cost you too much in drinks, will it? Depending what we have, of course. What's your speciality, Bobbie?"

"Green chartreuse!? Bobbie answers cheekily, lying stretched out on the grass beside me. I might have known she'd choose a drink of this colour, mightn't I?

"Bloody hell!" Simon complains. "Gonna cost us tonight, eh, sunshine?"

"You're mean – that's your trouble," Michelle gasps beneath him. "Come on, you great big hunk – get off me!"

Simon does as he's told, rolling onto his back again to sun himself. "Not what you said last night, is it me little passion flower? Didn't want me to get off then, did you? Not bloody likely – enjoying it too much, weren't you?"

"Shoosh!" Michelle implores him to remain silent. "Want to embarrass me?"

"That'll be the day, Michelle, my love."

So that's how we spends most of the afternoon – just lying around chatting, joking and sunning ourselves, don't we? The time soon goes by, and about five o'clock, Michelle expresses her desire to go for a ride on the minutia railway which is situated the other side of the Lido, ain't it?

"Come off it, gal!" Simon moans at her suggestion. "Bleeding kids' stuff, for crying out loud!"

Bobbie comes to her friend's support though. "Oh, don't be such a spoilsport, Simon. Sounds good fun."

"We'll put it to the vote. What you reckon, Henry – wanna go for a silly train ride?"

I jumps to me feet excitedly. "Yeah – why not? Getting too bloody stiff just sitting around here, ain't we? The pubs'll be open by the time we've finished our journey."

Simon drags himself to his feet. "I dunno, sunshine! Fancy taking sides with the gals. Can't trust a soul these days, can you?"

But through all his moaning, I think Simon enjoys himself on the railway as he sits up front of the train holding hands with Michelle thoroughly thrilled with the proceedings. "Pass down the corridor, please!" he hollers as we're chugging along through the woodland area, all the young kids that are on board, joining in with his jubilations, like.

Bobbie and yours truly is sitting at the rear of the engine, and it's not long before her soft hand is up to its old tricks again, caressing the inside of me leg. Know what I mean? Not that I'm complaining, am I? Not bloody likely.

"Thanks for supporting me and Michelle, Henry," she confides in me as the train rattles along the metal tracks that snake out in front of us.

"That's okay," I replies, grateful for this pleasant change of scenery.

"I'm really enjoying myself today – how about you?"

"Yeah – great fun. A day to remember, eh?"

"Pity we don't have a camera with us?"

"We'd have captured you all right – swimming with all your clothes on. Still wet, are they?"

"No – bone dry with the sun."

By this time we're on the second lap of our train excursion, ain't we?

"Mind the doors, please!" we can hear Simon shouting up front amidst wild laughter from fellow passengers.

We can see the engine driver – a red-faced, beefy bloke who's wearing all the proper gear – uniform an'all. Right giggle really.

"Feeling nervous about tomorrow, Henry?" Bobbie asks as we pass near to the lake, a water skier sweeping close by before zigzagging further out on the water.

"A bit – yeah," I confesses truthfully to her. "I'll be glad when it's all over now."

Bobbie's hand comes to rest in mine. "Good luck, anyway," she wishes me kindly. "I do hope things work out all right for you."

"Yeah – for either me or Simon, eh?"

"You mustn't think that way. Call it a woman's intuition if you like, but I'm sure you'll beat him, Henry."

"Hope you're right. I'd certainly like to win. Who knows where this Big Chance will lead? I wouldn't want to hurt Simon if I do though. But, as they say – all's fair in love and war, eh?"

She gives me John Thomas a little squeeze as the train pulls to stop alongside the wooden platform at the end of our journey. Bloody hell! What will she be doing next, I'm wondering?

We stroll out of the Lido in the direction of the car park where Michelle's car is situated. And you wanna see it. It's similar to Bobbie's, ain't it? But a different colour, yellow! Bright bleeding yellow! Unbelievable!

"Right! See you all later down the pub then, okay?" Simon says, looking in the side mirror of Michelle's car to comb his hair. "The 'White Fox'. We'll have the drinks all lined up seeing as Michelle's footing the bill."

And with that, they zoom off down the road in a cloud of smoke in Michelle's hot rod, don't they?

We follows on behind and eventually meets up with them at this here pub what Simon's on about. Nice place – homely, with a garden out back. We get our drinks and go sit at one of the empty tables on the lawn. There's a few other customers dotted about, whilst inside up at the bar it's quite crowded. Lido users mostly, thirsty, like ourselves after an exhilarating day.

"Great day?" Bobbie comments, lighting a cigarette. "Made a pleasant change."

"Certainly did," Michelle agrees.

I'm enjoying a nice pint of beer, ain't I?

"And we honestly do wish you every success tomorrow with Big Chance – the both of you, don't we, Michelle?"

"Yes – the very best."

Simon's busy puffing at a cigar he's just lit. "No punch ups over it, eh, sunshine?" he jokes.

"Certainly not, me ol' fruit," I agrees with him in a friendly manner.

"Wouldn't want that now, would we?"

"Can't have you two falling out over it, can we?" Bobbie adds in good humour.

"Too right, gal," Simon agrees. "Already had disagreements about my tie, ain't we? Don't approve of it, do you, sunshine? I'll tell you something though…The ladies certainly do, I can vouch for that, Henry, me ol' son. Go on – ask them what they think, why don't you? You'll get your answer there all right, I tell you. I mean, no risk – nothing, is there for 'em?"

I takes a swig of me beer, sensing an argument in the air. "Most gals want a family before agreeing to that sorta thing, I'm sure," I retaliate.

"I don't think you're a hundred per cent right on that score, sunshine! Not by today's standards at any rate…. Women's Lib an' everything. Half of 'em don't want bloody babies, if the truth be known. Too busy enjoying themselves, ain't they? No – a woman's place ain't what it used to be. Their roles have changed, see. I mean – nappies and washing – it's not for them these days. It's the truth, I'm telling you."

"Get away," I says, after his lecture to me. "A few maybe like that… but the majority wants kids and a home, I know. Only natural, ain't it? All this bleeding talk of sexual freedom – where's it going to lead to in the end?"

"I dunno, mate – ask the gals – it's 'em what we're on about. Ask them. Bet you any money they don't want it any other way, sunshine! Specially these two – see the bloody world and what's going on it, don't they? Ask if they're still virgins like their mothers were at their age? No, mate – not bloody likely."

"Well, of course we're not virgins!" Bobbie informs us emphatically. "What the hell! About time we girls had a bit of equality. Not that we're as black as you paint us to be, Simon; but I see no reason why we shouldn't have as much sexual freedom as you fellas in this crazy world we live in."

"Yes, I agree," Michelle, who had remained silent up till now, agrees with her friend's statement. "You men have it far too much your own way. Who do you think you are anyway?"

This statement is met with considerable silence from us here men folk, I can assure you. No stopping these bleeding women once they get started, is there? Best to keep one's mouth shut while they're in this present state of turmoil, wouldn't you agree? Know what I mean?

"I think that's your question answered, me ol' sunshine!" Simon addresses me finally. "Satisfied now?"

I finishes me beer. "No, I ain't then," I tell him firmly. "Mean to tell me that none of these gals want kids when they eventually do decide to marry – settle down, like?"

"Yes, I'd like a home and family when the time comes, of course I do," Bobbie informs me calmly.

"So would I," Michelle indicates.

"Well, you're not bloody likely to, are you…? Not with blokes like him around anyway. I mean – he can't accommodate you now, can he?"

"I think you're jumping the gun slightly, Henry," Bobbie accuses me. "After all, it's not every virile male in the country who'll be having this operation without first considering its affects very carefully, is it now? Those who decide to will probably be married men anyway – and they will have had their families. So you could say that they're contributing a service to society by their actions really. I mean – over population is a serious world problem, wouldn't you agree?"

Simon rises to collect our empty glasses. "You tell our Henry what it's all about, passion flower, while I go get us some refills."

"You can say what you like, but I'm convinced it's a free passport to permissiveness," I sticks with my opinion on the subject. "I mean – you don't even have to be married, cos there's blokes you hear about what ain't and still having the bleeding operation, ain't they?"

Michelle interrupts at this stage of the discussion: "Surely it all boils down to one's beliefs ultimately, doesn't it? It's a purely personal thing really, isn't it?"

So what chance do I stand, eh? I mean, three against one. "But I honestly believe it's wrong. I mean, handing out ties for Chrissake! What next, I wonder – Green Shield bloody stamps!"

"No – transistor radios!" Michelle smiles.

"Beg pardon?" I enquires, a little bemused by her sudden statement.

"In the East – they're giving them all transistor radios to have the operation."

Simon returns with fresh drinks. "Still at it then?" he asks, setting down the glasses.

"I read somewhere though that even these drastic measures to curb the birth-rate are causing problems for these nations," Bobbie enlightens us further.

"Good health everyone!" Simon offers a toast, raising his glass. "Here's to the jolly ol' chop and for all who go in for it!"

"Seems there's not enough people to now do the manual work out there," Bobbie continues with her commentary.

"Yes, I suppose they do rely on large families for labour don't they?" Michelle offers her opinion.

"Exactly!" I interrupt boldly. "Nature must take its own course. Interfere with that, and you are asking for trouble."

In the meantime, Simon is busy concentrating on his beer drinking, ain't he? "Oh, let's drop the subject for Chrissake!" he suggests. "It's all a matter of opinion anyway. Up to the individual finally, ain't it?"

So we all does as he orders and concentrate instead on our drinking, spending the rest of the evening in doing just that. It soon flies by, and before you knows it me and Bobbie are bidding Simon and Michelle farewell, ain't we? Cos Simon's gonna be journeying back to Michelle's pad, like. Seems she'll be leaving for Paris in the morning to spend a week there on a modelling job. All right for some, ain't it? Still, good bleeding luck to her.

"Hope you haven't forgotten about tomorrow, Simon?" I reminds him when we're all standing by Michelle's eye-catching sports car after having left the pub.

"No, cos I ain't. By the way – I'll make my own way there, Henry. I got all I need in passion flower's car here. So don't worry about me, and remember now, the flat's all yours, okay? Take care of him, Bobbie, won't you? Be seeing you then."

They pull away, leaving me and Bobbie standing on the tarmac watching their car disappear up the street.

"What now?" I sigh despondently, shoving me hands in me trouser pockets.

My companion sides up to me, linking her arm through mine.

"Back to the flat, I suppose?"

"Okay. You're the chauffeur."

"Let's go then."

We race back to Simon's place in less than fifteen minutes.

"You were in a hurry?" I question this illustrious beauty when we're sitting on the sofa sipping sherry.

"No point in beating about the bush, Henry," Bobbie confides in me, her hand clasping my knee.

"No, I s'pose not," I agrees, getting all hot under the collar. Bloody hell! Who wouldn't?

Then we're kissing, ain't we? Mmm... could she, as well. Leaves me gasping. Know what I mean? And her hand is all over the place, like, one in particular which is busy unzipping me, ain't it? Not that I'm complaining, cos I ain't, I can assure you.

Then, just as I'm about to break a bleeding blood vessel yet once again, Bobbie gets to her feet, pulling me up also. "Let's away to bed, Henry," she suggests, nibbling at my ear. I mean – what's a bloke supposed to do – refuse? Yeah – I'm sure.

And so to bed where we makes wild, passionate love, don't we?

You wouldn't credit it really – bloke like me making it with a top class model. Don't get me wrong. I mean, I wouldn't swap it for the world, would I? But me conscience starts to bother me, don't it? Not that I got anything to feel guilty about. Most fellas would jump at the chance. No, it's not that. It's Carol, ain't it? Starts thinking about her, don't I? I'm still very fond of her, you see. I dunno, complicated life we lead at times, you must agree.

Not that I needed to worry on this score, because on awakening the following morning, I discover that Bobbie has gone, ain't she? Not even as much as a goodbye. I dunno. Women! Who the hell can figure them, eh? Well, I sure ain't gonna try, am I? Cos today I've got other things on my mind, haven't I? It's me Big Chance day, ain't it?

So I grab a shower and shave before breakfasting, then spend best part of the day rehearsing me number for the Show. I bought meself a new outfit for the occasion – jeans and jacket, colourful shirt. I'll have me lucky beads draped around me neck, won't I? Yeah – just you wait – I'll show 'em all. Just so long as me and Simon can remain good buddies, whatever the outcome brings is all that really matters in the end though, ain't it?

Later that evening, feeling as excited as I've ever felt in my life before, apart from last night with Bobbie, that is, I lets meself and me guitar out the flat to make me way down to the good ol' BBC television studios.

Chapter 9

Upon arriving at the BBC, I'm shown to a dressing room where another bloke is busy getting make-up applied to his face by an attractive looking, young Make-Up gal.

"Good evening!" this here dame greets me, dabbing powder all over this geezer's nose. "You must be Henry Higgins?"

"That's me," I informs her, propping me guitar against a chair and sitting down.

"Be with you in a jiffy – just finishing our Calvin here, aren't we, dear?"

Calvin is a young bloke with long, dark hair. He's all geared out in evening dress, the bleeding lot. Wanna see him – you'd think he was attending a Buckingham Palace reception or something!

"This is Calvin Spicer, the other contestant in the Show tonight," the Make-Up gal enlightens me. "Calvin – meet Henry Higgins, another singer, like you."

Spicer shoots me a look in the mirror in front of him where he can catch a glimpse of me reflection, like. "Hello! Henry," he greets me politely.

"How's things?" I enquire with a friendly smile.

"Bit nervous – you?"

"Yeah – a bit."

"There! I think that'll do for you, Calvin," our powder-puff lady approves of her work, whisking a towel neatly away with a flick of the wrist from Spicer's neck. "Now you, Henry – if you'll sit yourself down here."

"I'm at your mercy, luv." I jokes with her, taking a pew in front of the long mirror.

"What type of song do you sing, Henry?" Calvin questions me. I can tell by the way his voice is trembling that he's feeling bloody nervous about the ordeal that awaits both of us. Well, least it makes two of us, don't it?

"Singing one of me own compositions tonight," I tell him with a certain amount of confidence. Don't want him to know that I'm suffering from a butterfly stomach the same as him, do I now? "I've called it Double-Cross Baby."

"Sounds interesting."

The Make-Up gal applies cream all over me face after donning a white towel round me neck.

"What will you be singing?"

"Oh, something a little more serious… The Desert Song – 'I'll Join the Legion'."

Bleeding good luck to you an'all, mate! I thinks to meself.

"Tenor, see. It's my kind of material. I wonder what sort of accompaniment they'll give me."

Oh, the full bloody treatment, mate, what else? I think again as this dame applies mascara to me eyebrows and lashes. I mean – what the hell does he expect – bleeding Mantovani orchestra or something for Chrissake! "Wouldn't know, mate, I'm sure. It don't worry me – accompanies meself on guitar, see."

It's then that the door bursts open and Simon comes stomping through. He, too, is wearing evening dress suit for the occasion, ain't he? "Watcha! Henry. Not late am I? Got held up, didn't I?"

"Hello! Simon," I greet him, pleased that he's made it. "Michelle get away all right?"

"Yeah, fine. I tell you – what a night!" Simon's looking at me in the mirror, and I can tell that he, too, is acting kinda nervous, like. The both of us know that tonight's the night – shit or bust!

"Say – I hope you ain't gonna doll me up like that, are you, darlin'?" he questions madam mascara.

"But of course," Miss Make-up informs him sweetly. "You have to if you're to appear on television. You'd look awful if you didn't."

"This is Calvin, by the way," I interrupt their conversation. "The other personality in tonight's Show. He is the 'Desert Song' man."

"Would you Foreign Legion it?" Simon can't resist the pun, can he?

Anyway, to cut all the dressing room chat, and to get on with the story, we shortly had to follow the geezer what was here when we first auditioned for the Show, old 'clapper-board', remember? We're asked to accompany him down this long corridor, ain't we?

"All right, are we, everyone?" he enquires after our welfare as we head off in the direction of the studio where this here Show is to take place.

"I've laid me a couple of gorgeous females since we last met," Simon boasts to him gleefully. "How about you – anything as exciting in your life?"

"Nothing so strenuous as your love life conquests, young man," clapper-board comments with a certain amount of distaste.

"How about you?" Simon asks 'Desert Song', who, by now, is looking a little white about the gills, despite his heavy make-up.

"N-no," the bloke stammers nervously. "Happily married man."

"Oh, God! Not another bitten the dust, surely?"

I'm sure this bravado from Simon is only to hide his true feelings of nervousness as we await the ordeal that lies ahead of us.

We halt outside some swing doors, beyond which, we're told, is the actual television studio. It's here that we are met by the producer, this Brian Goodchild geezer, white hair an'all.

"How are we all then, dearies?" he greets us with his usual effeminacy. "Nervous, no doubt? Yes – only to be expected. Never mind, even the best suffer from this. Now – just two minutes before count down, duckies! A few brief words… I'm the one who'll be introducing the Show tonight. All three of you will be sitting at the rear top end of the studio. You'll be mingling with the audience. Gives it all a touch of authenticity involving you in this way. Now – there's to be a special guest singer who'll appear on the Show…A Miss Pearl Stanley. No doubt you've heard of her? Yes? She'll be kicking the Show off so to speak after I've got rid of the opening formalities. Now, directly she finishes her number I then go on to inform the audience of the first of the artist's tapes to be played… The one you did at auditions, remember? Now I won't know in what order they are played; but directly they are, the camera will pan in on whoever that one is, okay? On completion of each individual tape, we'll monitor the audience's response to it, and the one to receive the highest volume of applause will be the winner. Got the idea? Now – are there any questions? "

Simon lights himself a cigar. "Yeah – will the Show be live?" he enquires.

"No, it's pilot. A decision whether or not it'll be given the go ahead comes later from various sponsors who've watched it. All right? Anything else?"

Yours truly and 'Desert Song' are too bleeding petrified to speak, ain't we? So Goodchild commences with the chat once more, don't he?

"Our pretty songstress will then perform another ballad for us, after which, lucky contestant number two's tape is played…Same thing again – camera shot of entertainer before recording audience applause. A comedian then follows by the name of Cocker Brown."

"Bet he'll cock things up!" Simon cracks.

Goodchild gives him the evil eye for this remark, obviously not amused. "If I was you I would save your jokes for when it's your turn, Blackwell," he advises him coldly. "Right… I think that's all you need to know."

"Hadn't you better give them instructions about the winner?" Clapper-board advises, hovering in the background, like.

"Yes, of course, how silly of me, most important. Now – whoever is judged to be the winner, should, at the appropriate time, walk slowly down the steps and onto the stage to join the Band there to give a performance of his act… Understand?"

We all nod our heads up and down like puppets to indicate that we do.

"Good as won the thing, ain't I, sunshine?" Simon boasts with self-assurance, blowing cigar smoke in the air. "It'll be champagne all round then, me ol' son, won't it?"

Calvin don't say a word, does he? Just stands there as if he's bleeding well messed himself.

The three of us then gets ushered through the door into the crowded studio beyond. The place is packed, ain't it? But the audience don't know who we are as we sit in amongst them at the back, do they?

Then, before we know what's really happening, this Goodchild geezer's jumping around on the stage below us introducing the Show, ain't he? A Band behind him swings into action.

"Good evening, folks!" he greets everyone with a friendly smile, a television camera zooming in on him, a large screen at the front of the studio showing us a huge close-up of him and the Band, like. "Welcome to Chance of a Lifetime! My name's Brian Goodchild…yes, and I'll soon be introducing you all to our three main contestants taking part in tonight's Show! They are here…! And they're raring to go, I can tell you!"

A camera seeks out us three suckers, showing us up on the monitor screen as the audience burst into spontaneous applause prompted to do so by some geezer standing to the right of stage who's holding a large board above his head with the word 'APPLAUSE!' written all over it in very large letters. We just sit there looking bleeding stupid, don't we? Scared to death really, ain't we?

Then old Goodchild continues his rabbiting. "But first, folks…! And to get the Show under way – we're very privileged to have with us in the studio tonight that well known talented jazz singer of international fame… Ladies and gentlemen! A big hand, please, for Miss Pearl Stanley!"

The APPLAUSE! board comes into action again as this coloured singer bounces on stage to swing into *Sweet Georgia Brown*, with the audience applauding her wildly. Us other artists sit admiring the talents of this sophisticated lady of song, at the end of which, we, too, join with the APPLAUSE!

Then the compere's in on the act again, ain't he? Going into a dialogue to explain what the Show's all about and of those participating in it, and of who will be the very first week's lucky 'Chance of a Lifetime' winner?

"And now, folks…! The moment we've all be waiting for! The first artist's tape to be played! Remember – it's you in the long run who'll determine by the volume of your applause which of the three you think is your particular favourite! Now…! Are we ready up there in the control room, yes? Good…! Here, then, is tonight's first Chance of a Lifetime tape for you to listen to!"

You can imagine how us three artists are feeling sitting up the back waiting to hear our own tape being played now, can't you?

And whose do you think is the first one up? Yeah – suddenly loud and clear comes the voice of our singing Desert Song friend to give us all his rendition of 'I'll Join The Legion – that's what I'll do'. We watches on the big screen as the camera shows a close-up of Calvin and of the surprised look on his face. We also see some faces of the audience and of their reaction to the tape.

At the end of the song, Calvin receives quite a generous ovation for his efforts.

"Thank you! Thank you…! That was our good friend, Calvin Spicer, folks! With his very rousing performance of a number from The Desert Song. Calvin is a postal worker from Bedfordshire. Marvellous voice, I think you'd agree."

At this point, Pearl Stanley is reintroduced to sing us another one of her classic numbers before the next tape, which is Simon's. His jokes make everyone fall about with laughter and his song at the end indicates a higher volume of applause than our Foreign Legion geezer got, don't it?

"That's it then, sunshine!" he says quietly to me as Cocker Brown takes to the stage to entertain the audience. "Leaves just you now. So good luck me son. And may the best man win, eh?"

I know he means it, cos he says it with such sincerity, like, know what I mean? Yet at the same time I seems to detect a note of despair in his voice, like he knows he ain't gonna win the contest. In which case, that leaves just me left in the running, judging by the audience's reaction so far.

Anyway, I'm sitting there shaking with bleeding fright waiting to go on, ain't I?

The next thing I know I can hear me voice loud and clear as it sings "Double-cross, baby – it's a double-cross…!" after Goodchild's introduced my tape to the audience. I don't look anywhere other than straight ahead of me, do I? Too damned frightened to do anything else really. "Cos you ain't nothin' but a double-cross!" the song finally concludes.

And you wanna know something? They seems to like it, cos everyone's applauding wildly, ain't they? They've made their decision, it would appear. It's me they've chosen. I'm their bloody winner, ain't I?

"Congratulations, sunshine!" I hears Simon next to me say.

"Yeah – congratulations, Henry," Desert Song shakes me vigorously by the hand. "You've done it!"

"Go on, Henry – get down on stage. They want you. Show 'em what you can do, eh?"

I feels myself rise to me feet and float down the steps toward the stage.

"Here he is, folks…! The young man you've voted as tonight's winner of Chance of a Lifetime…! A male model from Hertfordshire…! Henry Higgins…!"

Everyone's applauding like crazy, ain't they?

"…And here to sing his very own composition once again – Double- cross baby – is your Chance Of A Lifetime choice, ladies and gentlemen! Henry Higgins!"

So I sits meself down on this stool on stage and sings them me song once again, don't I? But with more confidence this time, see. Piece of cake now that me nerves have left me, ain't it?

Back in the dressing room afterwards, Brian Goodchild informs me that the BBC will be getting in touch to let me know if the Show will get the go ahead or not. I'm praying that it does, like, cos then this really could be my chance of a lifetime.

"I hope things go well for you, Henry," Calvin wishes me as we part company. He's looking well choked, ain't he? I mean, all the way up from Bedfordshire for what? Still, that's the way it goes. Back to being a postman, eh? Or the French Foreign Legion?

"So long, Calvin – bad luck, mate," I offers him my sympathy.

I suddenly become aware of Simon's absence from the scene. Where the hell's he got to? Come to think of it, I ain't seen hair or hide of him since the Show finished, have I? Hope he's not a bad loser, that's all?

So I gets changed and calls in at a pub round the corner for a celebratory drink to mark me new found fame. As I sit sipping me beer, I wonders to myself why Simon has taken off in such a hurry. After all, he could have stayed for a drink, couldn't he? Join with me in me good fortune, like? I dunno, p'raps it is sour grapes after all. I won't let it upset me though. He's had the same chance of winning as I had. Just that they liked my act better, that's all. Then again, maybe he has a date somewhere? Or perhaps gone back to the flat for something?

But when I arrives there a little later, there's no sign of him anywhere, is there? And for a bloke what's just won a TV Talent Show, I'm feeling just a little bit pissed off with everything, I can tell you. There's no one to share me excitement with, is there?

So, before going to bed early I phones me ma and informs her of the good news, don't I? "Let Carol know as well, will you?" I ask her.

"Of course I will, Henry. It's marvellous news! Well done, dear. She'll never believe it, will she?"

Before drifting off to sleep, my last thoughts are of my Carol, ain't they? Wonder what she'll think of me now then, eh?

Chapter 10

I don't see anything at all of Simon during the course of the following week, do I? He don't phone me neither to let me know what's happened to him, does he? I mean, if he's feeling sore cos of me winning the Show, well, then that's just too bad, ain't it? After all, I don't think I would behave in this manner if it was him that won the bloody thing now, would I? I'd be pleased for the guy, I know. Then again, maybe it's something else that's bothering him? But whatever, he should let me know of what the hell's going on inside his head. I sits in all week waiting for him to contact me, but nothing happens, does it? So getting fed up with me own company, like, and wanting someone to share with me to celebrate my winning this BBC thing, I decides to go home for the weekend to see me ma and pa and maybe a few other friends for a friendly chat and drink 'round at the local, don't I? I'm glad I does, cos what followed was an experience that brought me closer to me old man and to witness a side to him that I never knew existed and which made me look at him in a different light altogether. Plus, the fact that we are like one big happy family, as we all congregate in the back bar on Friday evening, all of them having finished work early for the weekend. By now, everyone knows about me good news with the BBC, don't they? Cos of Ma having proudly told them of what's happened, like.

"Gee! That's just swell, Hen…ree," Jason congratulates me in his usual Clark Gable manner.

"Great news, me ol' son," Stench agrees with his drinking partner, busying himself with a roll-up. "Have to get us some tickets so as we can all come to see you on the big night, eh?"

"Ye…eah! Don't wanna miss out on that now do we, fellas?" Jason's eyes light up at the prospect.

God help us! I thinks to meself at the thought of these two characters sitting in the audience. I mean – can you imagine? But then, they are me followers after all is said and done. They don't mean any harm, do they?

It's at this point that Tom Basset, the landlord of the pub, comments on a column he's reading from a newspaper from behind the bar. "I see Frank's in London to perform in three charity concerts at the Festival Hall starting tonight, Charlie," he informs me old man of this knowledge.

"Is he? I never knew that!" me dad exclaims in disbelief.

"Who's Frank when 'e's at 'ome?" Stench enquires nonchalantly amidst a haze of smoke from his Golden Virginia tobacco.

"Who else, but the one and only Frank Sinatra!" Tom enlightens our good friend. "Here with the Count Basie Band, ain't he?"

"It says all the tickets have been sold for all performances."

"Stands to reason, fellas – likes of you an' me don't have a hope in hell of getting in to see the likes of him now, do we?? Jason remarks sarcastically. "Them tickets are snapped up by all them high-class dames and gents of society long before Sinatra ever arrives in this little ol' country, I know? Besides which – if you ask me – the Mafia controls the purse strings to these concerts anyway? Well-known fact that the man's involved with the mob, ain't it?"

"It's never been proved," me dad jumps to the crooner's defence at this accusation from Jason. "Don't matter anyway cos he's still the best entertainer in the world by a long chalk."

You see – both me old man and Tom Basset are Sinatra's most ardent admirers and won't have a word said against him, will they? They have all his records and have seen all his films and know in detail all there is to know about the man. They even have monthly late night drinking sessions together with the singer's songs coming out over the loudspeakers in the bar, don't they? Sinatra Stop Outs, they refer to them as. Just the two of them, no one else. Yeah, they were Frank's followers all right and would dearly love a chance of being able to see the great man in concert, wouldn't they? Little hope of that though. It would be simpler, it seems, to obtain an audience with the Pope. I must admit, I quite like the man myself and admire his way with a song. Very versatile in all that he undertakes.

"We could wait outside the Festival Hall and tackle the ticket touts, Charlie?" Tom makes this suggestion to their dilemma.

"We could never afford their going price, I know," me old man confesses. "Charge the bloody earth."

"I honestly don't know what all the fuss is about over one blessed singer, for goodness' sake," me ma intercedes, somewhat agitated by the whole subject.

"Oh, cum on, missus," Jason interjects passionately. "The guy's an institooshun, for cryin' out loud. I mean – even the name "Frank Sinatra" conjures up a certain feeling of magic about it, ya gotta admit, lady."

"You tried phoning him the last time he was over, didn't you, Charlie?" Tom asks after pulling himself a pint of beer and coming 'round to join our company the other side of the bar.

"I certainly did," me dad confesses, obviously remembering the occasion. "Didn't have much luck though, did I? Maybe I should have another go now that he's in Britain again? Never know – I might get through to him this time?"

Jason's face grimaces as he finishes the remains of his scotch.

"Don't talk crazy, man. I reckon on all hell freezing over before you're ever likely to do that, kiddo. The guy's surrounded by mobsters and bodyguards all the time. You'd never get near the fella, I'm tellin' ya."

"It might be worth a try, Charlie," Tom ignores this statement from Jason, "I'm not sure, but I think I read that he's staying at Claridge's."

Me pa is pondering on these remarks from his pal when me ma, after finishing her stout, rises from the table.

"Behaving like a lot of bloomin' children, if you ask me," she pontificates. "You're all fully grown men, for goodness' sake! I'm off home for some peace and quiet. Make sure your father gets into no trouble now, Henry."

After Ma has left, me old man decides to do something about getting in touch with his singing idol, by asking yours truly:

"Perhaps you could phone Frank for us, Henry, and ask him for some tickets for one of his concerts?"

"I'm sure the man's gonna give time of day to speak with the likes of me now, ain't he?" I replies to his request, unable to believe that he's asked me to do this. "Talk sense, Dad, for Chrissake! Just wouldn't happen, would it?"

Jason's brown eyes light up suddenly. "I reckon he might pay attention to me, you guys. The accent an' everything – know what I mean? As one fella countryman to another, like?"

This suggestion is met with hushed silence for a moment, followed by a few sniggers from both Tom and me ol' man at the sheer preposterousness of it. Gotta admit though that our phoney American has got some balls to even contemplate such an idea really.

However, no one present takes him up on it, do they? Which is just as well when you truly think about it.

"Well, I think it's worth a try, Son," me dad continues to twist my arm on the subject. "He might just listen to you, being a teenager an'all? Flattered that he could still have a following from the younger generation, like. Know what I mean?"

"Yeah!" Tom Basset says enthusiastically, "I think you could be right. Come on, Henry – wotya got to lose?"

Stench's head appears slowly from behind a cloud of blue smoke at the far end of the table. "Only his pride, that's wot!" he says in obvious disapproval of their plan for me. Nice to know someone cares, ain't it? "Do yer own dirty work, why don't ya?"

But by the way, me ol' man and Tom is looking at me, I knows that they want me to agree with their request. And as Tom says, what have I got to lose anyway? Be a right laugh if I did manage to contact the geezer and secure some concert tickets for everyone, wouldn't it? Mind you – I think they're both crazy. I mean, two grown-up men behaving in this way is right barmy, ain't it? I could understand if they was a couple of teenagers idolising a pop group or something? I could identify with a desire of that nature as I could imagine doing it meself, I suppose.

"What exactly is it you want me to do?" I weakens finally.

"Thataboy!" me dad says excitedly at the thought of putting his plan in to action. "Pass him the phone over, Tom and let's get cracking."

The landlord reaches behind the bar for the phone and hands it to me.

"We'll need a London directory as well, please, Tom."

This is soon found and plonked on the table in front of me.

"Now what?" Jason questions with a wry smile creasing the corners of his thin-lipped mouth, amused, it would seem, at his friend's behaviour over this matter.

"Now, Henry is going to ring Claridge's in London to see if Frank is staying there, that's what", me old man informs him as he checks for this hotel's number in the book. "Here it is – you dial 01-629-8860, Henry."

Being the good boy that I am I do as I'm told, don't I?

"Good evening! Claridge's Hotel," a man's voice greets me almost immediately.

"Er, hello, yes – Claridge's?"

"That's correct, sir. Can I help you?"

I hesitate, feeling a right bloody idiot, I can tell you. "Yes, er, could you let me know if a Mr Sinatra is staying at this hotel, please?"

"Who, sir?"

"Mr Sinatra? Mr Frank Sinatra?"

"No, I'm afraid he isn't, sir. I understand he's at a private residence in Grosvenor Square."

"Grosvenor Square?"

"Yes, that's right, sir."

"I see. Well, thank you – thank you very much."

"My pleasure, sir."

I puts the phone down, hoping that this will be the end to any further plans to contact the singer; but I has a strange feelin' that somehow it won't be, don't I? Leastways, knowing me old man the way I do it won't, cos it's a safe bet to say that he won't let the matter rest at this point of the proceedings, I know.

"He's not at this hotel," I tells me dad and the landlord. "They say he's residing at a private address in Grosvenor Square someplace."

Both the old man and Tom look at each other thoughtfully for a few moments as they mull over this piece of information. I can see their eyes both light up simultaneously. Now what do they want me to do, I'm wondering?

"It's a clue to his whereabouts, that's for sure," me dad indicates with a smile.

"It sure is," Tom agrees with him enthusiastically, while Jason and Stench look on with avid interest from their positions in the background. "It's a lead, ain't it?"

"Yeah – all you gotta do now, Son, is ring enquiries and ask them to give you some phone numbers for residences in Grosvenor Square to try, ain't it?" Pa instructs me. "There can't be that many there, I know? Just tell them you're trying to contact Mr Sinatra, that's all."

"Just like that?" I question this madness.

"Ye…ah, just like that, man!" Jason jumps on the bandwagon.

"Tell them it's an emergency," Stench adds to the conversation, "of the utmost importance to find out where the bum is staying, like. Yer got that?"

I takes a deep breath, then gets back to the job at hand, don't I?

"Enquiries! Which town, please?" the operator's voice asks.

"London."

"Name an' address of people?"

I hesitate for a moment. "Well… I haven't actually got an address really. You see, I'm trying to contact someone who I know is staying in Grosvenor Square somewhere. I wonder if you could possibly give me the names of some buildings or blocks of flats that I could ring. Perhaps I could locate this person that way?"

A few seconds silence, before: "There's a Providence House in Grosvenor Square…"

"Providence House?" I repeat, writing the name down on a piece of paper that the landlord's provided for me together with a pen with the pub's name written on one side.

"And a McDonald House…"

"McDonald House… Yes, got those…"

"Britannia Hotel is listed…"

"No, don't want any hotels, thank you…"

"Have you the name of the person you're trying to contact?"

I takes a deep breath. "Yes, his name is Sinatra! Mr Frank Sinatra!"

"I see…"

At this point, everyone involved in this crazy scheme – that is – me ol' man and Tom, Jason and Stench, fall into complete silence at the mention of this celebrity's name. Their eyes are all staring at me, ain't they?

"Could I ring those two buildings you've just given me?" I continue further with me investigating.

"The trouble is there are hundreds of numbers listed under them, sir," I hear the operator say. "Ah, wait a minute. There's a Canada High Commission office here. Perhaps they might be able to help you?"

I didn't think so meself; but it was another number to ring, and who knows? "Yes, I can try it."

"You ring 01-629-9492. Wait though, I've just spotted a head porter's number at one of the other ones…"

Yeah, that sounded much better, didn't it? A head porter was far more likely to help me than anyone really. Even if Sinatra wasn't at this address, he might by chance know where he was hiding?

"That one is 01-629 – 2629."

"Thanks for your help, I'll try it," I jot these numbers down.

My companions all look at me with bated breath.

"Just a couple of numbers in Grosvenor Square, that's all," I put them out of their misery. "It ain't Sinatra's though." That would be asking too much, wouldn't it?

Me ol' man downs his pint. "Never mind, Son. Keep at it, you're doing fine, ain't he, lads?"

"You sure are, Henry," the landlord agrees with his friend. "Time for a drink, don't you think?"

"Sc…ar…ch on the rocks for me, Tar…m," Jason interjects, emptying the contents of his glass with the utmost speed, then wiping his pencil line moustache with the back of his hand.

Not to be left out, Stench gulps down the remains of his beer and utters: "Same again for me, guvna!"

With all our glasses replenished, it's time for me to get down to business again, ain't it? And to tell you the truth, I'm quite enjoying the challenge now that I've got into it. Well, it's a laugh, ain't it? The question is, which number to ring first?

"Ahh reckon on that Canadian one ma...self," Jason gives his expertise on the matter.

"Just leave young 'Enry to get on wiv' it in 'is own way, you daft bugger," Stench reprimands our Mr Gable with severity.

I picks up the phone and dials that first number, then wish I'd rung the porter's one instead. This Canada think was obviously a business building on its own somewhere in the Square. Sinatra was hardly likely to be staying there now, was he?

"Hello! Canada High Commission," a woman's voice speaks in me ear.

"Yeah, I wonder if you could help me, please?" I ask. "I'm trying to locate someone who is residing in Grosvenor Square. The operator seems to think that you might be able to assist in this matter. I'm trying to find the address of a Mr Sinatra. Would you happen to know of this?"

"I'm afraid not, sir... He wouldn't be here, that's for sure. The American Embassy might know?"

"The American Embassy?"

"Yes, that's right. If you hold the line a minute I'll find their number for you..."

"Thanks very much," I notices Jason straining at the bit to be in on the act after hearing mention of this particular Embassy. Maybe he could put in a good word for me with the American Ambassador?

"Yes, here we are. You ring 01-499-9000 for the Embassy."

I wrote this down. "Yes, I got that. Thanks for your help."

"Thank you. Good-bye."

I rings the new number.

"American Embassy," a woman's voice drawls in my ear.

"Yeah – I'm trying to contact Mr Sinatra," I speaks to this voice- bravely, my own not quite as hesitant now as when first attempting these lines of enquiries.

"Hold the line, please..."

At this stage Jason finds the intrigue of it all too much for him and has to sit down next to me in an effort to overhear the telephone conversation, bending his ear close to the phone.

"Welfare, can I help you?" another woman's voice enquires.

"I'm trying to find a Mr Sinatra…" I asks again.

"Mr Sinatra is stopping next door to the Embassy at number 35 – 37 Grosvenor Square…"

I hurriedly write this down. "Thank you very much."

I slam the phone down. "Got it!" I sigh joyfully.

"Great stuff!" both me old man and Tom exclaim together ecstatically.

"Things are looking good, man!" Jason drawls as he pops a stick of spearmint into his mouth which he then commences to chew rapidly.

Stench curses to himself as the excitement of it all makes his hand shake so much that he drops tobacco on the floor from a roll-up he's in the process of preparing.

"Now all we want is the man's room number?" I indicate to our overzealous group.

You could almost hear their minds ticking over in the silence that follows my statement.

"Why not try that porter geezer?" Stench suddenly comes out with to astound us all. "'E might know, mightn't 'e?" By now he has successfully manufactured a fresh roll-up to pollute the atmosphere with.

"Why not, indeed?" me old man praises Stench's ingenuity. "Good thinkin', me ol' son."

"Yeah, well done, Stench," Tom agrees. "He might well be the key in solving our problem?"

Not to feel left out, Jason makes known his opinion on the subject also. "Well, stands to reason, you guys, that the good ol' Yoo S of A Embassy would know of this fella's whereabouts now, doh…nit? Car…men sense really, ain't it, me ol' buddies?"

No one pays any heed to his comments though, least of all Stench who is once again engulfed in a haze of smoke at the end of the table. "I still don't know who this Hank Sultana geezer is you're all goin' on about," he mumbles out the corner of his mouth.

"Cool, man, don't let it worry ya," Jason keeps his drinking partner in the dark to save giving him an explanation, which, even if he did, would leave the old boy still none the wiser.

I dials the porter's number, don't I? "Hello, 2629."

"Hello, is that the building next door to the American Embassy?"

"This is 2629," a man's cockney voice repeats.

"Yeah, I know that," I says to the geezer. "But is your building next to the Embassy?"

"You tell me – is it?"

"I don't know, that's what I'm asking you?"

I realise I've gone about this in totally the wrong way, ain't I? "You see, I'm trying to contact Mr Sinatra?"

"Well, he's not here," the man grumbles, and hangs up on me.

"I think he's blown it, man," Jason frowns, while the others look on in silence.

I contact the operator once more. "Hello, enquiries, which town, please?"

"London. Thank you."

"Name and address of people?"

"Well, I've got the name. You see, I'm trying to trace someone who I know is stopping at 35-37 Grosvenor Square."

"Are you the same gentlemen who was on the line earlier?" the operator enquires.

"Oh, hello, yes, I am," I informs her, recognising the voice.

"Did you say 35-37 Grosvenor Square?"

"Yeah, that's right."

"I've got the head porter's number that I gave you. He could probably help."

"No, he can't. I rang him. He said Sinatra wasn't there."

"He never gave you any other information then?"

"No, he just said that he wasn't there, that's all."

"I'm not sure who can help you then."

"How many flats are there in this building?"

"Let me see…There's three, six, twelve, eighteen…twenty four altogether."

Which one of these could he be in? I'm wondering "Can you give me some names listed for these flats?"

"I'm not supposed to really, sir," the operator explains sympathetically. "Perhaps if you were to know one of this particular gentlemen's associates that might be listed in the book?"

For Chrissake! How on earth was I to know any of Sinatra's friends?

"Sorry, no, I don't," I sighs helplessly.

A prolonged silence follows. "If you had a flat number you could give me, then I might be able to help. Otherwise…"

"Try flat 17," I give to her in desperation before she hangs up on me.

"Number 17… yes, here we are… a Miss Peach is listed for that one."

"Miss Peach?"

"Yes, and her number is 01-629-2241."

I writes all this information down. "Thanks a lot for your help. Maybe she might help?"

I dials this newly acquired number with my captive audience all looking on with avid interest as this latest stage of development begins to unfold.

"Hello, 2241," a refined woman's voice answers.

"Hello, there," I says calmly, with no trace of nerves now, this continuous phoning becoming quite natural to me. "Could I speak to Mr Sinatra, please?"

"Who?" a confused, but friendly sounding voice queries the name.

I knew that I had to try and make this lady think I had been genuinely given her number for Sinatra's, and convince her of this by sounding sincere in what I was about to say. "Mr Sinatra – could I speak with him, please?"

There was a slight pause. Then: "I do think you have the wrong number. This is 2241, I am Miss Peach."

"Oh," I says, trying to sound surprised, "I was given this number to contact him with. This is 35-37 Grosvenor Square?"

"Yes, that is correct."

I can feel me old man and the rest of them almost breathing down me neck by now.

"Obviously I've been given your number for Mr Sinatra's," I continues me conversation with the lady in question. "I wonder why? He is staying at this address, isn't he?"

"Yes, as a matter of fact he is. There's been quite a commotion over him in the corridor today."

"Has there really? He's quite a character, isn't he?"

"Oh, a charming man – absolutely charming."

Commotion in the corridor? I thinks to meself as a policeman might when investigating a crime. If this good lady occupies flat number 17, then it might well be true to deduce that the allusive Mr Sinatra should be on the same floor as she, wouldn't it?

My dad elbows me in the ribs. "Ask her for Frank's room number, for Chrissake!" he splutters, getting all hot under the collar with the realisation that there might just be a chance of contacting his singing hero.

"Ye…ah, ya almost there, man," Jason emphasises. "Don't mess it up with this dame now, buddy boy."

"Keep calm, Henry," the landlord advises, unable to hide his excitement as well.

Stench also has something to say. "Get Miss Peaches an' cream to tell old Frankie Sinbad that we're on our way up to 'ave a drink wiv' 'im in 'is flat, okay?"

Choosing me words carefully so as not to sound too obvious with me request, I continues with the telephone conversation. "This is a nuisance," I commence, "you see I have to get in touch urgently with this man by tomorrow night. Now, you say that I have the right address, but the wrong telephone number? In fact, the wrong room number, it would appear?"

"Yes, it would seem so."

"You wouldn't happen to know his room number, would you?"

"No, I'm afraid not, I'm awfully sorry."

Her reply makes me wince, don't it? Now what the hell am I supposed to do?

"I wonder who could possibly help me in this matter. You don't know of anyone, do you?" I'm asking this woman in desperation as I look at the disappointed faces of me old man and

Tom and their pals as they hear my response to these questions I'm putting to her.

A prolonged silence. Then: "You could ring Jones, the porter, he might be able to help you."

"Jones?"

"Yes."

"I see. Well, thanks very much. So sorry to have bothered you."

"That's quite all right."

I hangs up the phone rather dejectedly. After all, this Jones fella wasn't all that over the moon when speaking to him on the subject the last time, now, was he?

"He's the geezer you rang earlier, ain't he?" Tom Basset remembers.

"Yeah, an' a fat lotta good it done then, dinnit?" Stench remarks cuttingly, puffing his cigarette.

"You gotta try him again," me old man insists, not wanting to give up on his quest in getting in touch with his great idol.

"I'm tellin' you fellas, the guy's unreachable," Jason states knowingly, draining his glass dry of the last drop of scotch. "Be easier to break into Fort bloody Knox, man, an' that's a fact, take it from me."

I must admit that I don't feel like pursuing this idea any further meself, do I? But I sees that me dad is hell bent on exploring every avenue along the way before admitting defeat. So, to keep him and his lifelong friend, Tom, happy, I dials this porter's number again, don't I?

"2629! Can I help you?" the tone of voice sounding a little more amicable this time.

"Yeah – I think perhaps you can. You see, I'm trying to contact a certain person who is staying at your address. A resident of yours – a Miss Peach – says you might possibly know this gentleman's phone number?"

"Did she now?"

"You are Jones the porter, aren't you?"

"No, I'm not, Jonesy's gone off duty."

I bites me lip. "Oh, has he? Well, maybe you can help? You see, I'm trying to reach a Mr Sinatra. Do you by any chance happen to know his telephone number?"

"No, I'm afraid I don't, sir. His number is strictly private."

"But he is staying at this address, isn't he?"

"Oh, yes, he's here all right – room 14."

"Thank you, room number 14, you say?" I double check, barely able to conceal my joy at this discovery.

"Yes, that's correct, sir."

"Much obliged, good-bye to you."

"Good-bye, sir."

I hang up. "I got his room number!" I shouts jubilantly.

"Hooray!" me old man screams with delight at the news.

"Great stuff, Henry," Tom echoes in similar high spirit.

"Yeah, ya did well, kid," Jason congratulates me with warm approval.

Stench wipes his mouth with the sleeve of his jacket after finishing the contents of his glass. "Who knows – we might just be 'avin that drink wiv' the geezer after all then, eh?"

I decide to phone enquiries again to see if they can give me any information on Sinatra's room number, don't I? This I immediately do, only to be told that it is listed as ARTANIS PRODUCTS LTD, and that the number is unobtainable. No hope in that direction then.

"Wait a minute," me old man says suddenly, scribbling something on a piece of paper with me pen. "Yeah, I thought so. Look – ARTANIS is SINATRA spelt backwards, ain't it?"

"So it is," Tom agrees with his friend's deduction after examining it.

Jason offers a wry smile at this news. "Which only goes to show you ain't neva gonna get thru to the guy, are ya?"

"Never you mind, 'Enry," Stench comes to the defence of the plan. "It also shows that you're on the right road in tracking 'im down, that's for sure. Keep plugging away – you'll get there, I'm sure of it."

But I wasn't quite so optimistic now, was I? I mean, if we didn't have a phone number to contact the man with, what use was there in continuing further with the project?

"Tell you what – we could try working a sequence of numbers from that of Miss Peach's and maybe come up with something?" Tom suggests as a last option to our predicament.

"Yeah – wotta we go to lose?" me dad agrees with a smile.

"Not a hope in hell, kid," Jason tries putting the kibosh on the idea.

Stench is quick to put him in his place though. "Yer won't wanna come wiv' us for a drink with him up in London then once we've cracked it, eh?"

Anyway, after trying as me old man suggests, we don't have much success along these lines, do we? Cos this system only gets us through to some employment agency in Oxford Street, a dry cleaners at some other place, and a fella residing in Pinner. So we finally decides to call it a day with regards to contacting the man, and resign ourselves to the fact that the only way of getting to see him at one of his London concerts is to travel up to the Festival Hall to approach the ticket touts to see if they can help us out, like.

"Told ya so, buddy boy," Jason is gloating at our failed exploits. "Could've saved yaselves one helluva lotta time if yood a listened to me now, wouldn't ya?"

The rest of us ignore his remarks, don't we? As we sit contemplating our next move in the saga, it hits me, don't it? "We could write the man a note to explain our dilemma and leave it with that porter geezer at Grosvenor Square to give to him?" I comes up with. "Then maybe he might leave some tickets on the door for us. Never know – it might do the trick?"

The others sit there in complete silence as they mull over my suggestion. Even old Jason is passing no comment, is he, as he muses with the others on its chances of success?

"Yeah, why not," me old man finally gives it his approval. "Can't do any harm, can it? Besides which, it'll be a chance for us all to have a night out together, won't it?"

The landlord goes along with the idea also, as does Stench as well, which only leaves Jason, our rolled up, shirt-sleeved friend for his opinion in the matter. "Ye...ah," he mumbles approvingly, nodding his head up and down. "It might juss work, man, it might juss work."

So we all spends the next half hour composing a letter between us to the American singer in an effort to help further our cause in seeing him perform live at his Saturday midnight concert. We all contributes to it, saying how we had tried contacting him by phone with a view of securing tickets for one of his concerts, and of how we'll be travelling up to London in Stench's old van in an effort to get in to see him. We mentions also of how much we appreciate the work he does for charity, and that if there is any chance of him leaving five tickets at the door of the Festival Hall, we will be all eternally grateful to him.

"That should do the trick," me old man says with confidence, adding his signature to the letter along with the rest of us.

Tom stretches his arms above his head. "No one can say that we haven't tried now, can they?" he yawns.

"What's the plan of action gonna be then, fella's?" Jason enquires, as if he were in a Clarke Gable military movie preparing for battle to save his country, like.

"'Ark at 'im," says an annoyed Stench at his friend's sudden show of interest from this latest development. "'E didn't want anything to do with the plan a minute ago. Now he wants to mastermind the whole bleedin' thing, don't he?"

"All right, all right – let's not row about it, you two," Tom disciplines the pair of them.

Then me old man offers them the following advice: "Look – all you two's got to remember is to turn up looking the part for this very special occasion, ain't it?" he preaches to them. "Jacket and tie, the pair of you, else you can both stay behind, okay? In the meantime, one of you can go get the drinks so that we can raise our glasses to my lad, Henry, here for all the hard graft he's done on the phone this afternoon. Well done my son."

They do as me dad tells them, and I feels happy with meself, not only for receiving this praise, but because, to be perfectly honest, I quite enjoyed the challenge they set me, didn't I?

Anyway, we decides to all meet outside in the pub car park at eight o'clock the following evening, and from there journey up to Grosvenor Square in Stench's work van to deliver our letter to Mr Sinatra before going off down to the Festival Hall to negotiate some tickets for his Show just in case he won't leave any for us there later. Be great if he does, like, but it's a pretty tall order to expect of him, if you ask me. Of course, Ma thinks me and the old man are barmy when she gets to learn of our plan, don't she?

"You should know better at your age than to go gallivantin' half way across London with this half-baked idea of yours," she lectures Charlie just before we sets off on our expedition. "An' you mean to tell me that you've not even bothered to contact Carol since arriving home, Henry?" she turns on me with vengeance on discovering this truth, and that I have no intention of doing so either because I tells her that I don't reckon it's my place to do so, but hers, if she wants to talk to me. Not that we have anything to discuss now that she's made her bed and has to lie in it as far as I'm concerned, right?

Be that as it may though, we all duly sets off on our journey to Grosvenor Square shortly after eight that Saturday night after meeting up with the rest of the gang in the pub car park, where Tom, the landlord, and Jason, and last of all, but by no means least, our driver, Stench, along with his van, who, by the way has made a tremendous effort with his appearance, as has his fellow friend, Jason, who both look immaculate and hardly recognisable dressed as they are in their Sunday best for the occasion.

"Just look at these two, eh?" Tom comments on their transformation as he steps up into the van.

"Yeah, even their own mother's wouldn't know them, would they?" me old man congratulates the pair of them on their turn out, joining Tom in the passenger seat, while Stench takes up his position behind the steering wheel, leaving yours truly to scramble in the back with Jason to sit on a hard wooden bench.

Thirty five minutes later, we roll into Grosvenor Square and park the van on the far side of the road opposite the American Embassy, me old man feeding some coins into a parking meter to cover our stay, while I go to deliver our note to Sinatra, and the others take the opportunity to stretch their legs. I suppose we look somewhat conspicuous all piling out the van in a residential area such as this; but what the heck! We had come with a specific purpose in mind, and we weren't going to back down now no matter what. Besides, I knew it meant a great deal to me old man and Tom to at least make the effort along these lines to see their hero, bizarre as that might appear. If the plan failed, then it wouldn't be for lack of trying now, would it?

"Sure you're all right doing this, Son?" my Dad then asks me with some concern as we amble along in the direction of numbers 35–37.

"I… I'm fine," I replies a little hesitantly at the thought of the task ahead of me.

"If ya want, I can do it," Jason offers his services in this direction as he swaggers along the pavement. "His hench boys won't put me off, I tell ya."

"'Ark at 'im, 'e's a bleedin' joke, ain't 'e?" Stench retaliates to this suggestion. "Run a bleedin' mile yer would if threatened."

We arrive at our destination in the Square.

"Don't get cold feet on us now," Tom says light-heartedly as we stop outside the entrance to the building.

"We'll leave it to you then, Son," me old man speaks for the rest of them as they abandon me to get on with the job at hand.

It's at this stage that I experience a butterfly stomach and wonder to meself what the hell I'm doing here in the middle of London. After all, the chances of this little experiment ever succeeding are virtually impossible in my reckoning. But then, I have to remind meself that I'm only doing it cos of me dad and old Tom anyway, and if it makes them happy, well…

With this thought in mind, I takes a deep breath, pushes open the entrance doors to the block of flats, and marches in.

A short, shiny-faced, uniformed man immediately advances toward me across the thick, soft, red carpet of the lobby. "Yes, sir, can I help you?" he asks politely.

I hands him the envelope containing our precious letter to the famous celebrity. "Could you deliver this to Mr Sinatra, please?" I bravely begs of him.

"Yes, I'll make sure he gets it, sir," the porter takes it from me.

I fakes a cough. "Shall I wait for a reply?"

"I'm afraid Mr Sinatra won't receive this until later, sir."

"Won't he?"

"No, sir."

"Is he not in at the moment then?"

"No, sir, he went out about ten minutes ago and won't be back until the early hours of the morning."

"I see," I says, annoyed at having just missed him. "Well… you will make sure he gets my letter, won't you?"

"Yes, I'll make certain he does, sir."

I walks out of the building, turns left and bumps straight into me old man and the others who have obviously been waiting just round the corner for me to emerge.

"Well?" they all enquire together.

"He's not there," I inform them of the bad news.

"Watcha mean, not there?" me dad demands an explanation.

"Yeah, he's gotta be there," Tom insists.

"Got the right address, ain't we?" Stench enquires.

"Where the hell is the guy then?" questions Jason.

"He's gone out," I tells them all dejectedly. "Won't be back till the early hours of the morning by all accounts so I left our letter with the porter."

We all stand around looking at each other, wondering what to do now that our plan has been thwarted. It was to be expected I suppose really. Nevertheless, it still leaves us feeling somewhat at a loss as to what our next move should be? If indeed, there will be one now under the circumstances.

Not wanting to admit defeat though, me old man suggests the following: "Well, I reckon we should all go for a drink someplace and decide on our next course of action, don't you?"

Everyone is definitely in agreement with this, especially our two smart friends, as we all troop off to find the nearest pub.

"It's certainly puts pay to tickets from Frank as a non-runner, that's for sure," me old man concedes sorrowfully over a pint of beer in this here drinking house that we soon locates without too much difficulty ten minutes later.

"Well, it was a bit of a lar…ng shot, fellas, ya gotta admit," Jason tells us in a told – you – so manner, whilst enjoying a scotch.

Stench lights a roll up after nearly consuming half his pint of bitter in one gulp. "I reckon we're on a 'idin' to nuffin' comin' up 'ere," he moans from behind a cloud of smoke.

"My sentiments, exactly," Jason, for once in his life, finds himself agreeing with his old buddy. "Crazy idea in the first place, man."

However, both me old man and Tom have more positive feelings on the subject, don't they? Which is only natural really, considering it was their brain-wave idea in the first place, weren't it?

"Well, I think we should all go off down to the Festival Hall and see what's doin' there with the ticket touts," me dad espoused vigorously.

"Yeah, so do I," Tom supports this suggestion. "After all, we're up here now, what have we got to lose?"

Stench finishes the remains of his drink. "Oh – 'bout a few 'undred quid in my estimation, that's all," he surmises with a chuckle.

"An' that's jus for one ticket, yoo may be sure," Jason adds with a shake of his head.

I can see by the looks on their faces that me old man and Tom both know this to be the truth, but obviously don't want to throw the towel in at this stage, do they? So, feeling sorry for them, I goes along with their train of thought, don't I, even though I know deep down our chances of purchasing a ticket each at a price we can all afford, is practically nil?

"I say – we have come this far – so let's go the whole hog an' see where it leads, eh?" I put to them all with forthrightness.

My utterances along these lines seems to do the trick, for there are no words of opposition to the idea from them, is there?

"Let's have another drink first though, shall we?" me old man smiles with approval at me for supporting him in this way.

"I think we'll all go along with that, Charlie," Tom agrees with his friend's motion.

Matter of fact, we have more than just the one drink before leaving the pub, don't we? We got plenty of time, see, cos the concert don't start till midnight, so we makes the most of the opportunity afforded us, like. Not that we consumes too much, mind. Just enough to put us all in the right frame of mind to tackle those ticket touts later.

So we arrive in force at the Festival Hall about an hour before the show commences, after Stench has parked the van safely in a car park nearby. The first thing we notice is the large amount of people that are gathered outside the rear of the building behind the metal barriers lining the pavements. There is also a noticeable number of police present around this area as well, with dense crowds forming on the walkovers above.

"Would ye have a ticket to sell us?" a red-faced Irishman asks me as we stands idly by observing the scene. "Give ye a good price for one, sure I will?"

"No, we're looking for some ourselves," me old man tells the fella as we watch him walk away to accost other people for this request.

"That's a tout looking for tickets to buy and sell back," Tom informs us knowingly as a couple of taxis draw up at our rear with doors slamming. "I'll go see what price they're asking."

We look on with interest as our landlord engages in a conversation with a dark-suited tout. We notice also the lucky devils who have tickets and are walking round to enter the Hall to take up their seats in good time for the start of the concert.

Then Tom arrives back to re-join us. "Five pound bloody tickets for seventy pound a time – that's what they're askin'," he passes on this information to us.

"What!" I gasp in disbelief. And here we are with barely fifty quid between us. Bloody joke, ain't it? We don't stand a chance, do we?

With heads bent low, we slouch off in the realisation that our chances of ever seeing this man Sinatra are now all but dead.

Then we hear some fella shouting: "Frankie!" as he leaps the barrier in quick pursuit of a shiny-white Mercedes Benz that glides into view, the strong arm of the law though swiftly bringing the guy to a halt as the car, which we can only assume to be Sinatra's, disappears along a partly concealed tunnel to the left of the building and out of sight.

"We even missed him arriving," me old man sighs disappointedly.

"Yeah, there ain't a lot goin' for us at the moment," Jason says despondently.

"Come on – lets go round the other side," Tom tries cheering us up.

Here, it's all happening, ain't it? Jostling crowds, ticket-touts, the police, doormen; sleek automobiles arriving with their film star passengers, pop singers, the old, the young, the silks, the furs. And it's here that we stand watching, envious of the lucky ones gaining admission, sorry for the unlucky ones being escorted back out on forged tickets, among these, a young lady, who, we are told has parted with fifty smackers and her diamond engagement ring to go see this man Sinatra. Crying hysterically, she is ushered from the building to re-join the rest of us outside, the time on the clock of Big Ben away to our right slowly nearing midnight, the hour when the Basie Band would swing into their opening number.

And still we hang around hoping for a miracle to happen to enable us to see the Show. But no such miracle is forthcoming it would appear, is it? There are a few more late arrivals, most of the crowd disappearing now, until finally there's just a handful of us left outside locked doors.

"Come on, Francis Albert!" someone cries, hoping, no doubt, that the man himself will leave word for us unfortunates to be let in. But no such word comes, does it?

Then another person shouts: "You can actually hear Sinatra singing from up here!"

So we all follows like sheep, climbing the stairs that eventually lead us out onto a walkway where you can look right into the inner shell of the Hall through large, glass windows. Off to our right we can see silhouetted against the darkened sky, various well known London buildings, Big Ben and the Houses of Parliament being the most prominent of these, the time now 12-thirty am, precisely.

We notice a dozen or so people leaning over a railing looking down at some cars parked below. It's where Sinatra's white one was driven along earlier and where it is now positioned, ain't it? Suddenly, we can hear Frank's voice wafting out to us at intervals with the Count Basie Band just about audible in the background.

"At least we can hear the geezer, even if we can't see him," Stench remarks impatiently.

"Yeah – I s'pose its better than nothin'," Jason, for yet once again in his life, has to agree with his buddy.

I can see though that both me dad and Tom are far from happy with this arrangement as we gaze down below us at the singer's impressive looking automobile in the roadway. But what else could we do? We had backed a loser in coming up here in the first place, hadn't we? So all we could do was to sit tight, so to speak, where we were, on the outside looking in, and hear brief snatches from the great man's repertoire. Unable to see him actually perform these though left us feeling somewhat humiliated in not having gained admission, hadn't it? And to make it even more frustrating for us, there were prolonged silences when we neither heard Sinatra's voice or the sound of the Basie band.

We endured this situation for about thirty minutes before me angry old man hisses: "This is no bleedin' good, is it?" and storms off in a right bloody huff.

Of course, we all follow him, don't we? None of us knowing where the bleedin' hell we're goin', like, but vainly hoping we may find some way of getting in. We all return minutes later, cursing our ill luck at being among the least fortunate without tickets.

"Whatya reckon then, fellas – shall we call it a day?" Jason suggests this option to us.

I peers up at the tall, long, white building standing in front of us like some huge fortress designed to keep us out. Surely, after all our efforts, we didn't deserve this fate, did we? Yet here we were, kicking our heels, our patience almost exhausted, and with the time slowly ticking by.

"What time is it?" me old man snaps impatiently.

"It's one fifteen," I informs him hurriedly.

Another hour and the concert would be over.

"Surely there must be some way of getting into this place?" our landlord growls with hostility.

I glances up at the building again, then, looking down, I notice some steps leading to a door to the left. I hurries down them, beckoning the others to follow. At the bottom a double door faces us. What if we could open these? I'm thinking to meself.

"Here!" I says excitedly, trying to prize them apart with me fingers. "See if we can force this open."

All five of us is about to put this plan into action, when, from up above, we hear someone whistle at us. Looking up, we finds a security geezer eyeballin' us from an opening in the wall, motioning for us to move away.

We climb back up the steps, the figure above now having disappeared back into the shadows of his garret.

"It's a bloody fortress, that's what it is!" me dad says in a frenzy.

"Yule get us all locked up if yer not careful," Stench aims at me angrily.

"Don't be such a goddamn yella-belly, man," Jason accuses his friend.

Sinatra's voice floats out to us again with his renditioning of the song Ol' Man River becoming audible intermittently. The early morning air has become quite chilly now, and as I look off to the left, I can see a row of arched lights on the near embankment opposite the Festival Hall reflecting in the water of the river Thames. I also notice Big Ben's time showing 1-30 precisely.

"I think we've missed the boat," I reflects sorrowfully, shoving me hands inside me trouser pockets for warmth and hunching me shoulders as a cold shiver runs through me.

"It certainly looks like it," Tom is in agreement with my statement. We all strain our ears in an effort to listen to another song from Sinatra, but we hear nothing. Even this pleasure is now being denied to us, it seems. In reality, I'm not all that bothered, am I? It's me old man and Tom who I'm feeling sorry for, cos they'd set their hearts on seeing their idol tonight, ain't they? After all, it might be the last chance they'll ever have? I mean, the man isn't getting any younger, is he, and he may not pay these shores a visit again?

Realising their chance to be slipping away from them, me old man says: "Come on – lets 'ave anuva go at that door!"

I checks to see if our friend is still keeping an eye on us from above. I don't see him anywhere though.

So, swiftly and quietly we make our way back down the steps again, don't we? After a great deal of clawing with our fingers at the door in an effort to prize it open, we don't seem to meet with much success, do we?

"It's no good," I whispers frantically. "It won't budge."

We have another go. Still no joy.

"Watch me bleedin' fingers, will yer!" Stench hisses angrily at us. We glance above. Our security fella is still absent from his post. "This time then," me old man murmurs softly, grabbing hold the bottom of the door with Stench.

I wedges me fingers securely in between the middle, while Tom and Jason grab the top as we all pull together, grunting and groaning as we do so, like, with the bottom of the door bowing out till I thinks it's going to snap, don't I? And then suddenly, she goes with a loud crack, the force of which knocks old Stench off his feet and onto his backside, while the rest of us steady the door and gaze above. It's all right. No one seems to have seen or heard the commotion. We hurry through the open door, gently closing and bolting it behind us.

We're in, ain't we? Then, after looking at each other for a moment, we slowly begin climbing the stairs.

As we tiptoe up and round the winding steps, we can hear Frank singing and Basie playing off in the distance, both becoming more prominent with each new step of our ascent. The stairs seem to go on forever, until finally, the excitement inside of us becoming almost unbearable with the singer and Band loud and clear in our ears, we come out at the top, where another set of doors confronts us. Pausing for a few moments to catch our breath from our long climb, me old man then gently pushes these open and we all march bravely forward, only to find another pair directly in front of us barring our way. These are obviously the final obstacle for us to overcome if we are to gain admission to the Concert Hall below, ain't they? Some tactful thinking is required at this stage, I'm thinking, as we could ruin whatever chance we might have of seeing Sinatra if we went about it the wrong way. I mean, we didn't want to get thrown out of the place after having coming this far with our venture, did we now? I think we must be all feeling the same way cos we just stands there in this here lobby frozen to the spot, don't we? I catches me dad's eye and gestures to him that I will take a look inside the Hall through a crack in the door. He nods his head in agreement with this, while the others, I notice, is all wearing petrified expressions on their faces, ain't they? Probably thinking that our exploits will see us all finally landing up in jail for breaking and entering the place, like. I must admit, the thought had actually crossed my mind. But to get back to the job at hand.

I peers through the opening in the door with me heart pounding wildly as I see a packed audience sitting in a partially darkened Hall watching the great man perform down below in front of them. I notices a green EXIT sign visible to me on the far wall opposite. I can neither see Sinatra or Basie from this position, frightened to open the door in case the bright light above us in the lobby becomes noticeable by doing so.

Then the audience is applauding Frank as he finishes his song Come Fly with Me.

"We better stay here and just listen," I recommends to everyone excitedly above the loud applause from inside the Hall.

"Yeah, I think you're right, Henry," me old man agrees with me suggestion. "We don't wanna run the risk of getting chucked out, do we?"

Jason has other thoughts on the subject though, don't he? "Jeeze, fellas – ya mean to say we come all this way just not to see the guy after all then?" he groans indignantly.

"What yer expect, yer muffin head," Stench retaliates strongly, "a bloody seat on stage or sumfin'?"

"Will you be quiet!" Tom reprimands the pair of them as the applause dies down from behind the closed doors. "The show'll be over soon. Then we can make our entrance, can't we, cos it won't matter then, will it? Not before though, okay?"

The applause fades away.

"Everyone agree?" Tom asks again, lowering his voice.

"Course we agree," Stench whispers back.

"Yeah, if ya say so," Jason grumbles quietly to himself in the corner.

So here we stands, listening to Frank as he sings his old favourites, Got You Under My Skin, First Affair, Road To Mandaley, Lady Is A tramp, our feet tapping, our bodies swaying to the rhythm of the big Basie Band. Then, with the time showing

2-15, and going in to his song, My Way, we know that this is Frank's closing number, don't we?

"Surely we can't go without seeing the man," I whisper frantically, as I lean forward to pull the door ajar slightly to peek through into the Hall. Then I sees him, don't I? He's standing erect on the stage, microphone in his hand, his immaculate evening suit shining in the bright spotlight, the musicians of the Band directly behind him. So this is the legendary Frank Sinatra? I thinks to meself, stepping back to let me dad and the others have their view of him.

Me old man, I notices, has this strange look in his eyes, as does Tom, and even Jason and Stench, all of them, in fact, captivated by the presence of this great entertainer and of the affect he has on everyone privileged to be here tonight, meself included.

With his final number nearing completion, we can contain ourselves no longer, can we? Cos we get this uncontrollable desire to be present with the rest of the audience when Frank finishes his song. We had nothing to lose now anyway, had we? So I pulls open the door and we all make our grand entrance into the Hall, finding ourselves situated at the top right hand corner of the building with the audience just below, and Sinatra and Basie further down on the stage. We joins in with the cheering and wild applause that has erupted all 'round the Hall for Frank as he takes a bow at the conclusion of his performance.

"We bloody well did it! Didn't we?" me dad remarks with pride at our remarkable achievement above the noise.

"We sure did!" Tom exclaims excitedly, responding with a loud whistle.

"Betcha life we did, man!" Jason boasts, a broad grin on his face.

Stench, who, up till this week has hardly heard of this American singer, is standing with the rest of us and proclaiming at the top of his rather uncouth voice: "'Oorah! We luv yer, Frankie! We luv yer!"

So, what had seemed the impossible, we had indeed achieved, as we stands there joining in with the rest cheering and applauding this man as he walks off stage, only to be brought back on again by the tremendous ovation being given him by his faithful followers. And then finally we see him take Count Basie by the hand and lead him out front as they both take a last bow before disappearing off stage together.

We then hurries down the stairs at the end of it all, thoroughly content with the way things have worked out for us. We may not have actually seen much of the concert, but we have been present at the finish, haven't we? We hang around with countless others to catch a glimpse of Sinatra driving away in his chauffeur-driven car, not before he looks up to give everyone a friendly wave first though.

And so we makes it back to our old van, talking on the way like excited school kids about our eventful evening. As I said at the start, it was an experience I'll never forget. I don't think any of us will really; but to be fortunate enough to have shared it with me old man, was really something, I can tell you, knowing how much it meant to him, see. No doubt it will be a talking point for many years to come, especially in the local boozer once everyone has come to know of it, like.

We moves off on our homeward journey, all of us sitting in silence to commence with, each with his own personal thoughts regarding the events of our night out in London. It's Jason though what breaks this quietness after having pondered on these events, like.

"Tell ya what, fellas," he drawls, "I think if yood've left the Sinatra negotiatshunn' to me ah reckon ah could've persuaded him to join us in havin' a drink togetha', that's for sure."

Stench sees it another way though, don't he? "'Ark at 'im – 'e's a right bleedin' dreamer, ain't 'e?"

Then, as we rumble along over Westminster Bridge with a full moon shining down on us from above, me dad suddenly exclaims with the utmost joy: "Whateva' – the fact remains that we achieved what we set out to do, didn't we?"

And Tom, seated next to him, agrees wholeheartedly with his friend's observation, don't he? And sums it all up by saying: "You're dead right we did, Charlie. I guess you could say that Frank has always done it his way all right, but there's no doubt about it – we most certainly did it ours, that' for sure, didn't we?"

With the old van coughing and spluttering, Stench sets about the task of driving us safely home, don't he? While the rest of us endeavour to get some shut eye before dawn breaks as we leave the city of London behind after a very memorable day.

Chapter 11

Any notions I might have had of making the big time and perhaps, like Mr Sinatra, of having fans breaking in to see one of my shows live was hardy likely now because of a letter I receives from the BBC the following week informing me that this Chance Of A Lifetime thing is not being pursued any further, is it? Knocking it on the head, ain't they? I dunno – after all you go through – only to see it fizzle out in this way, well, it's just not on, is it? All one's hopes dashed to the ground probably because some old geezer up there decides to pull the plug on it. Makes you sick, dunnit? The only positive thing to emerge from it is an artist's fee for appearing on that pilot show, ain't it? At least I got something for me troubles, I s'pose. Naturally, I'm disappointed at this outcome, and feel sorry for me family and friends. like, especially Carol. And what about old Tarp? I can see him now – revelling at my big chance going by the wayside. But then, it's not my bloody fault, is it? He won't see it that way though, will he? He'll look at it as more reason for my Carol to stay with successful him and I-told-you-so attitude, I know. Be hard to face them all now, won't it? But then, the show must go on, as they say. There is always this here modelling lark, ain't there? Almost finished the course for it now. Who knows – perhaps good fortune will shine on me in this game? I got this big fashion show what the Agency is arranging for us newly fledged models to appear at coming up next week, ain't I? It's being held at this posh London hotel somewhere. I'm told that there will be some agents floating about on the lookout for new faces. Never know – might catch someone's eye? Hope so, as it could mean another string to me bow, like. Besides, I'm getting tired of running around for Simon and doing what I'm doing for him. Anything's better than that, I know. You might like to know that I'm not seeing much of him these days. You see, he took it bad, losing to me on the Big Chance. Not that it makes much difference now, does it? Nevertheless, he did take it hard. He breezes in now and again to hand me his parcels to deliver. We don't have much to say to each other on these occasions. At the moment he's shacking up with some dolly from the Elephant and Castle. Something seems to be bothering him lately. Don't know what precisely, but he's definitely not the same happy bloke I first met, is he?

Anyway, the following week I takes meself along to this hotel to appear in this fashion show what I've been on to you about. It's quite a big do, with gals taking part as well as a number of us novice chaps from the Charm School, like. The fellas from the Press are all there, ain't they? Also a panel of judges from various fields of the modelling profession to assess our true potential, if any. The premise is that if we score enough points then we will automatically qualify to become fully fledged male models, won't we? Just like that, eh? Who knows – I may even bump into our friend Bobbie again through the course of my work? That's sure to be great fun.

So I shoots along to this hotel close to Leicester Square for this modelling show, don't I? In the meantime Simon's filled me in with how I should act and behave, ain't he? "Just wear what they tell you to and glide along the catwalk in them for the panel to see – you'll be all right, sunshine!" he assures me before adding with a mischievous look in his eye: "By the way – a word of advice. Target any of the female judges present there. Really play up to them, plenty of smiles and pouting of lips – sex appeal, yer know what I mean? It'll pay dividends with their markings, I'm tellin' you, mate, okay?"

"Yeah, sure," I promises Simon, who, by the way won't be there to support me. Got something on with this new bird, ain't he?

Well, the Show proves to be very popular, cos the place is crowded, ain't it? Not an empty seat to be found anywhere, is there? Bit frightening really, as us models gets shown to our dressing room to get changed into whatever clobber we've been allocated to wear. Yours personally is to show off a rather snazzy

131

sports suit, ain't I? I feels quite comfortable wearing it, a proper Jack-the-lad, like. The other fellas are attired in a variety of different designs, more suits, casual wear. One geezer is been asked to parade around in swim and beach apparel. Rather him than me, mate, I can tell you. Mind, it's a giggle, ain't it?

There's some luscious looking dames participating in the package. Not that we gets much chance to mingle and chat with them, like, cos we're all too busy changing and rushing on and off the catwalk, ain't we? I'm feeling nervous; but after a while I soon settle down and find I'm quite enjoying the Show. To accompany our movements there's background music being played which I find very soothing indeed. I haven't forgotten Simon's words of wisdom concerning the women judges, have I? And I immediately begins eyeballing one of them, this middle-aged brunette who reciprocates by offering me a warm, friendly smile for my efforts, don't she? I reckon old Simon knows what he's on about in matters of this nature all right. I receives a generous round of applause for me efforts, a great deal of this coming, I might add, from a circle of me friends what I've invited along to the Show and who are sitting in front to left of the stage sipping glasses of complimentary sherry being handed out to everyone by a group of waiters specially for the occasion. Right bloody laugh, ain't it? Mum and Dad's both there, in company with Tom, Jason and old Stench from out the boozer. Dad's brought 'em along for a night out, ain't he? With my permission, of course. Tom seems to think though that by allowing both Jason and Stench this favour, it could lower the tone of the place and maybe affect me chances for consideration in the modelling game? But I refuse to think along these lines, and consider them among my friends, as indeed they are of me old man and that it's no problem as far as I am concerned. After all said and done, they are our friends, ain't they? And want to be treated as such, don't they? So that's that on the subject, ain't it? Anyway, they certainly all seem to be enjoying themselves, especially the sherry part of it, like. I did ask me mum to try and persuade Carol to come along also; but she's busy going off to some function with Mr bloody Tarp, it appears. Shame, cos I think she would have enjoyed the Show, especially me prancing about on the catwalk. Mr Mayor couldn't make it either –

attending a cricket club dinner, I'm informed. But Mum says that they all send their regards and best wishes.

I'm pleased to say that I passes the model Show with flying colours and with ample points awarded me to qualify for the profession, don't I? Afterwards, in the dressing room, this tall geezer with a large cigar stuck in his mouth, comes round to see me.

"Ray Tandy –" he introduces himself, shaking me vigorously by the hand, "model agent!"

"Hullo, there," I greets him, changing into my normal clothes again, "Higgins – Henry!"

"How do you feel about me representing you, Heneree? I reckon we could work well together, a young, handsome chap like you? My reputation's good… have quite a number of other male models on my books, all doing very nicely, thank you very much. Plenty of work around at the moment. Usual fee – ten per cent… wadya say?"

I jumps right in with both feet, don't I? I'm in no position to refuse such an offer, am I? "Sure, why not," we shakes hands on the deal.

So that's that! Am now a young model with an agent, all within a span of a couple of hours. Magic!

To celebrate, I takes me family and friends along to this pub in Piccadilly for a drink.

"Great noos, Henree," Jason congratulates me, knocking hell out of a scotch on the rocks. "Be seein' ya up on that big screen afore long, buddy boy, yoo bet!"

That's confidence for you. "Who knows, Jase?" I comment joyously at his remark from my position up on cloud nine as I sip a glass of cool beer. Or is it cloud seven, I can't remember?

"Lets 'ope sumfin' comes of this modellin' lark then, eh, 'Enry?" Stench, whose becoming harder to recognise these days owing to his smart appearance at these social gatherings, remarks.

Me parents, who, I'm sure, are bewildered by all these goings on in me life at the present moment, sit quietly enjoying their drink, and pass no comment on these proceedings, do they? While Tom is more business-like in his thinking, ain't he? And can obviously see potential at making financial gains with this recent development for me, can't he? "Big money to be earned at this modelling game, Henry," he assures me knowingly. "Be careful not to let this randy – Tandy agent geezer rip you off though."

"If you ask me, it's all a bit of a mystery," me mum finally makes herself heard, a worried expression visible on her wrinkled brow. "After all, I thought it was only girls who went in for this sorta thing? They'll be calling you a sissy next, our Henry, you see if they won't?"

Me dad also comes out of his shell on the subject. "No they won't – don't talk silly," he comes to the aid of me defence, like. "Very 'onourable profession in my opinion. An' 'ighly paid, I might add. We neva 'ad jobs like this when we wus young, did we? Go for it, 'Enry, while yer can. Might not get anuva chance if yer don't."

We spend the rest of the evening like this – talking, arguing, drinking. It's all in good fun really though. No harm meant by any of the remarks made, I'm sure. We all stays till closing time. Then we grab a couple of taxis to journey along to Euston Station just in time to catch the last train home, with yours truly alighting at Harrow to make me way back to Simon's empty flat to call it a night after a very memorable day indeed, me only regret being that my Carol hasn't been around to share it with me.

Chapter 12

One Monday morning about a week later I receives this phone call from me agent, Ray Tandy, don't I? "Hullo, Heneree! Can you ride a horse, me ol' son?" he hurriedly enquires of me in an enthusiastic manner.

"Can I what?" I asks in disbelief at this request, thinking the geezer's flipped his lid, like.

"Dead serious, Heneree, got some work for you if you can, ain't I? Down at Southend."

"Doing what, for Chrissake?"

"Cigar-ad. Requires some galloping along the sea front on horseback. Reckon you can handle it? Good monee involved…"

"Bloody hell!" I gasps, taken aback somewhat by this unusual first piece of modelling work being put my way. I mean, I've never ridden a bloody horse in me life before, have I? A donkey, when I was a kid on holiday with me parents down at Clacton, that's all. Not really the same though, is it? Or ain't it? Who's to know it weren't an 'orse? Besides, I can't afford not to have a go, can I?

"Yeah – sure, I've ridden horses before," I lies to Ray convincingly, I think. Then, really jumping in with both feet again, adds with confidence: "When do they want me for it?"

There's a slight pause from me representative at this point, pleased, no doubt with my decision to take on the job, and, no doubt, at the thought of his commission from it also.

"Right choo are, then," he breathes a sigh of relief down the phone.

"Camera crew's meeting by the Pier at mid-day. Casual wear's required. Pair of jeans – shirt. Okay, me son?"

"Yeah, okay, got it."

"That-a-boy. Just do exactly what they tell you an' you'll be all right? I'll post your fee on to you when received – less my ten per cent, of course. Give 'em your best now, Heneree, an' so long for the time being."

"So long." I hangs up.

Me very first modelling job then, eh? Wonder what me folks an' Carol an' everyone will think when they see me on telly sitting astride some white stallion galloping along the beach at good old Southend then? Bet Tarp won't bloody well like it, that's for sure, will he? Just have to see where it all leads, won't I?

So I journey's along to this favourite coastal resort amongst the cockney clientele there to meet up with the television crew to participate in this here commercial, don't I? An' would you believe it – in no time at all they has me riding across the mud flats on this frisky white mare, don't they? Which at one stage I has to jump down from to light up this particular brand of cigar to indicate how much I am enjoying the perishing thing. Truth is, it nearly chokes me to death, don't it? The wonder of it all is I manages on film a first take, so everyone is well pleased with me efforts, ain't they? So me very first modelling assignment is a huge success. Least, with me it is. I'm not so sure how the general public will react though, am I? And it's them that has to be convinced to go out and buy the product now, ain't it? Anyway, it sure beats peddlin' porn for old Simon, don't it? Being as it's all been filmed down at Southend, it's gonna hold fond memories for me, I'm sure. And with Carol, too – if she ever manages to see it, that is. She probably won't recognise the place, cos you don't actually see much of the surrounds in the advert other than the sea with the tide rolling in and out and me there on top of this horse riding along. No doubt it'll appear as if it all takes place on some golden beach in the South of France somewhere. It ain't though, is it? If people only knew. Right laugh, innit? Each time I'll view it though I'll always be reminded of the time me and Carol made love there, won't I, right there on the beach? I wish she was here with me now to share me moment of glory, like, and perhaps maybe recapture our evening of passion. But she ain't, is she? And I'm wondering to meself whether or not she might now be experiencing something similar with that lavatory man, Mr Tarp?

Even the thought of them together like I had been with her makes me blood boil, I can tell you. Deep down though, I believe Carol is still faithful to me, don't I? Not like yours truly, who betrayed our love with Miss sport's-job gal, Bobby, ain't I? That was only to get back at Carol for taking up with Tory Tarp though, weren't it? Well, it's all water under the bridge now, I s'pose.

During the course of the next six months I find sufficient commercial work for television to keep the wolf from the door so to speak, don't I? Anything from toothpaste ads to bleeding breakfast cereals. I find if I just kinda act natural and speak whatever lines I has to correctly and with conviction – that's if I have any, like – then everyone seems happy, specially the sponsors, ain't they? It's not as if I'm ever going to be nominated an Oscar for this line of work now, is it? But it pays the rent, and quite well at that. And whilst on that subject, I'd like to inform you all that I'm no longer Simon's errand boy, am I? I tells him straight that I don't wanna do that sorta thing anymore, do I? He takes it all right and understands my reasons for jackin' it in. He knows that deep down I never liked doing it anyway. Not that I ain't grateful to him for putting this work my way, mind. Let's just say that I feels a great deal more comfortable without it and won't have to worry what people might think if they really knew what I was up to, specially me folks. He still pops in to see me occasionally, Simon, that is. After all, it's his pad, ain't it? He's far too preoccupied though with his latest gal to pay me much heed these days anyway, ain't he?

"Hear you're doin' all right with the commercials, sunshine?" he comments one day after I've informed him of me decision to quit doing his line of work for him.

"Yeah, regular work," I smiles contentedly, really pleased that I don't need to rely on his help anymore. "How you been keeping – don't see much of you these days, do we?"

He seems to be somewhat distant in his manner, don't he? He's certainly not the Simon of old, that's for sure. Has a real worried look about him somehow, don't he?

"I…I'm fine," he's trying his hardest to assure me. But I know there's something wrong, don't I? Cos he just don't look right as his face is all drawn, and he's lost one helluva lot of weight.

"Nothing wrong, is there, Simon?"

"Hell no – should there be?"

"Not really. Just wondered, that's all, not having seen you around?"

"Yeah, well, I can explain. Got a new angle going at the moment. Takes up a lot of me time, like. Makin' good money at it. No, don't you worry about dear ol' Simon, sunshine. Plenty of strings attached to my bow, see, ain't I?"

I'm pondering on what he's telling me, not wanting to pry into his business, yet at the same time, genuinely worried that he's hiding something from me. After all, if I can help in anyway, I will now that I'm standing on me own two feet. That's what friends is for, ain't it? I mean, if it wasn't for Simon I don't suppose I'd be involved in modelling, would I?

"What you into now then, Simon?" I enquire tentatively, hoping the tone of me voice won't betray how concerned I actually am for him.

He deliberates somewhat before attempting an answer to me question, like. Then, speaking quietly and almost as if from the corner of his mouth with the suggestion of secrecy about his actions, replies with a wink of his eye: "Films! sunshine."

"Films?" I repeats, unable to grasp the full meaning of his statement.

"Makes 'em meself now, don't I? Has me own production company with no shortage of gals and fellas wantin' to participate in 'em."

"What sorta films you talking about, Simon?" I'm fearing the worst possible scenario here, ain't I?

"What do you think?"

My fears are now substantiated by his remark.

"Blue films, you mean?"

"Blue, black, yellow – what's the difference, sunshine? So long as there's money in it, I don't care, do I?"

"You can't be serious?"

But by the expression on his face, I know that he is, like. Bloody hell! What next, I wonder?

"What if you get caught?" I puts to him to show him how concerned I am for his welfare.

He ponders the seriousness of this question for all of one second.

"No chance. Got it all well-arranged, ain't I? Keep tellin' you – no need to worry about dear old Simon."

Famous last bloody words, ain't they? Cos a month later Bobbie turns up at the flat informing me that she has some terrible news about him to relate as she collapses on the sofa with a horror stricken expression painted all over her pretty face. "Do you think I could have a drink, please, Henry?" she sighs despondently.

I pours the lady a good stiff one, wondering to meself what on earth Simon's gone and done to make her so distraught. "Here!" I hands her the glass, sitting down beside her. "Now – what has happened?"

Bobbie takes a good swig of the whisky, her face grimacing as the alcohol hits home. "I... I don't know how to tell you this, Henry..." she stammers.

"All right – let me guess. Simon's been arrested? The police have him down the station on a corruption charge – that it?" I'm almost convinced this is what's happened, to him, ain't I? Silly sod.

"I only wish it was as simple as that, Henry."

I can tell by her tone of voice that something is definitely wrong and that I'm not helping matters any for her by treating the subject in such a light hearted manner. If, indeed, these suspicions I have can be classed as such, like? "Come on, Bobbie – tell me – what's wrong?" It's my turn to sound serious now.

She finishes her drink, then, plucking up courage and coming straight to the point, says with a trembling voice: "He's dead, Henry – Simon's dead!"

It's almost as if a sledgehammer's hit me, ain't it? And I'm left shocked and speechless. It's quite a while before I manages to finally utter despairingly: "What do you mean, he's dead? He can't be!"

"It's true, I'm afraid... Gassed himself. They found him in this girl's apartment – the police... They had to break the door down."

"B-but when? Why? He was only here just recently."

Its Bobbie's turn to console me now, ain't it? We're both in a bit of a state, I can tell you. I mean, who wouldn't be? It's truly very hard to comprehend news of this nature, that's for sure. It's my first experience with this sorta thing, losing a friend, someone who's been close to you.

"Yesterday," Bobbie is sobbing, "they found him yesterday morning…"

Bobbie repays my compliment of a drink by pouring me one, which I'm grateful for, hoping it will dull the pain I'm feeling with this knowledge of Simon's loss under such tragic circumstances.

"What the hell did he wanna go and do a thing like that for?" I'm angry and searching for an answer. It is at this point that I begins to cry, don't I? After all, we were pretty close. Admittedly, we had our differences – but who doesn't? What a way to end it all though. Doesn't bear thinking about, does it?

After I regains my composure, Bobbie then starts filling me in with some facts concerning Simon's lifestyle that she thinks I should know about. It seems he got himself mixed up with a right bleeding crowd by all accounts. Apparently the police received a tip off with regards to his home made movie exploits, don't they? That's not all either. Drugs are involved, ain't they? Well, I mean, obscene films is one thing; but drugs? No, I don't hold with that sorta thing, do I? Even if he was my friend, like. Bloody hell!

"A very troubled young man if the truth be known," Bobbie concludes sympathetically.

"Yeah – you could say that," I have to agree with her. "But whatever? He could have phoned or something, let us know his problems? Could've helped maybe? It's such a waste of a life if you ask me."

"Makes one feel so helpless, doesn't it?"

"I still can't believe it, Bobbie."

"Nor me."

We sits there in silence, both with our own personal thoughts on what's happened, the pair of us embarrassed with the outcome of Simon's actions if the truth were known. What is one supposed to say or do when a friend commits such a dreadful act as this?

"Does Michelle know?" I finally break the silence.

"No, I've yet to give her the news," Bobbie deliberates thoughtfully on this unpleasant task, lighting herself a cigarette. "You see – she's only recently married… I don't want to upset her with this tragic news; but I suppose I will have to eventually, won't I?"

We continue to drink in silence, both of us withdrawing into our own individual shells as we contemplate privately on the sudden death of our friend. It's really knocked the stuffing out of me, I can tell you. I know Simon ain't exactly been himself lately… but bloody hell! I never in a million years ever thought this would have happened. It's Bobbie what finally breaks this eerie wall of silence between us, ain't it? "I'd like to ask a favour of you, Henry?" she addresses me quietly.

"What's that, Bobbie?" I replies to her request, grateful really for this respite to take me mind off Simon's awful suicide.

"I wonder – do you think you could put me up for the night? It's getting late, and I don't particularly relish the journey back to my place."

I get to my feet. "Course you can, luv. And thanks… thanks for coming over to tell me about Simon. It couldn't have been easy for you. I really do appreciate it."

"It's the least I could do. I mean, you were pretty close – you two. By the way – the funeral service is this coming Tuesday at Harrow Crematorium. I'm not sure if I can make it. I have an appointment in Bristol that day. I will try my best though."

"I see."

We spends the rest of the evening by just quietly doing our own thing, don't we? Bobbie occupies herself by rummaging through some of Simon's belongings. She comes across a collection of his long playing records which she then plays for us both to listen to. Wanna hear some of them. Unbelievable! I never thought Simon's tastes would be along these lines, I know. I think Bobbie's quite surprised too, because on the turntable and filling the air with rapturous sounds are compositions from such renowned classical geezers as Beethoven, Brahms, and Mozart. I mean – fancy ol' Simon goin' in for that sorta stuff, eh? Then, later, as Bobbie is preparing to go to bed, she uncovers some paintings lying on top of Simon's wardrobe, don't she? Reproductions, like, but of artists such as Van bleedin' Gough, Rembrant, Constable and likes of these geezers, know what I mean?

"Seems our Simon was a bit of a dark horse, Henry, don't it?" Bobbie remarks, admiring these works of art what she's lined up against the wall.

"You can say that again, luv. He certainly never let on to me that he was, well... an intellectual." I'm feeling quite bewildered by it all really, ain't I?

"And take a look here!" Bobbie draws me attention to a bundle of books hidden behind the sofa. "Looks as if our Simon was also the studious type... Open University course books... Foundation course in the Arts and Humanities... Did you know he was into all this type of stuff, Henry?"

"No, I didn't," I answer in astonishment at learning this latest revelation concerning Simon. Just shows – we didn't really know the fella at all, did we? But then, do any of us ever truly know one another? Makes you wonder, don't it?

So we call it a night, with Bobbie using my bed, while I bunks down in Simon's. Seems funny... A beautiful dame lying right beside me practically, and neither of us is in the mood to do anything about it, are we? This terrible news has affected both our thoughts and feelings to the extent that it makes you feel that there's a lot more to life than just sleeping around, don't it? Even Simon knew this all right, didn't he? Judging by what we've learnt tonight about him at any rate.

I awake the next morning to find Bobbie's up and flown, ain't she?

There's a note on the table by the bed. *Have a lot on today, Henry, so will have to dash. I don't know if we'll ever meet again. Sorry I can't make Simon's funeral. You do understand, don't you? Good luck with your modelling. Love always —Bobbie. x*

Tuesday duly arrives and finds me attending Simon's cremation, don't it? It's a sad business, cos there's barely a handful of people present, is there? I don't know any of them, do I? I'm not even certain that he's got any family or relatives. If he has, well, he's never mentioned them to me, like, has he now? Anyway, those of us what is there just sit quietly as we listen to a sermon being given by an expressionless-faced vicar of sorts. Some elderly bloke with his shoulders hunched is seated alongside me on my right. Could be he's Simon's old man, maybe? I never does find out though, do I? After the sermon and a couple of hymns that nobody joins in with the vicar's excuse for singing, cos none of us has ever heard it before, the pine box with Simon's remains then descends out of sight as the organist plays a final hymn to conclude the ceremony. It's at this point that I has a lump come to me throat, and tears in me eyes as I realise I won't be seeing Simon any more. Least, not in this world at any rate. Poor ol' Simon. I mean, what did he achieve in life at the end of it all, eh? Nothing much, was it? Pub comic? Male bloody model? Porn bleeding pusher? But then I suppose it's not really an honest picture of the guy, is it? After all, he was trying hard to educate himself, weren't he? And he certainly had an appreciation for art and music, that's for sure. No, I guess that nobody really knew Simon, only Simon himself. So bloody sad though – going out the way he did.

Leaving the chapel and not even bothering to say good-bye to anyone, I heads for the Station to catch a train back to the flat, don't I? On the return journey I'm wondering to meself what the hell happens now about this? Do I just take the place over, or what? Have to investigate this, won't I?

Chapter 13

Sure enough, the landlord soon pays a visit to inform me that I can stay on at the flat if the previous financial arrangements he had with Simon is to my satisfaction, like. I goes along with this, don't I? However, before departing, the geezer tells me that there's two month's rent outstanding, and would I be so good as to clear these arrears prior to me taking over the pad, like. I dunno, fine bleedin' start this is, ain't it?

It's not the only debt Simon's left behind neither, cos I'm also paid visits by other business associates of his wanting to know if any arrangements have been made with regards to recovering money owed to them by him. Hell – what have I let myself in for, eh? I mean, there's camera equipment what he's never paid for, ain't there? A few hundred quids worth here at least. So I squares this up, don't I? Well, I can't leave debts like this hanging over him now, can I? There are numerous other bills he's neglected to pay as well. It's a good job I'm now earning a bit to wipe the slate clean for him, ain't it?

I'm soon to discover something else though that I really didn't bargain for. You see, there's these two gals from the Elephant and Castle what pays me a visit to enquire whether I can put them up for a spell – just till they find themselves some suitable accommodation, like. What next? I wonder.

"We've nowhere to go," one of them pleads. "Simon said to call on you anytime we might need help, didn't he?"

"We wouldn't ask, but we're really desperate, luv," the other begs. "We've bin kicked out of our place, see?"

"Yeah – the landlord's a right so an' so, ain't he?"

It's then that I remembers where I've seen these two characters before. Simon's funeral, weren't it? So, being the soft-hearted fool I am, like, I tells them that they can stay at the flat until they sort themselves out.

"Thanks a million, darlin'!" they both utter as they takes turn to throw their arms around me to show their appreciation of me kindness toward them. That's me though, ain't it? A good, kind-hearted Christian citizen.

So they departs to go fetch their belongings to move in, don't they? The positive side to all this I suppose is that they can help out with the rent, can't they? I mean, they don't seem all that bad a type. Just cos they pose in the altogeva to make a few blue films, it don't make them evil now, does it? Far worse things happen, I know. And shortly after they moves in, I'm about to find this out, ain't I? Cos you know what? None of 'em is working at the present moment, are they? And by the looks of it they have no bleedin' intentions of doing so neither. It's muggin's here who's footing the bills, ain't it? Yeah, working like a right nut, ain't I? There's plenty of it around, see, which, as you can well imagine, keeps me agent happy, that's for sure. He's highly delighted, ain't he? So would you be if you were creamin' off ten per cent of me earnings, I know. Still, I s'pose he does find me the work in the first place, don't he?

No, me business life's in a healthy enough state. It's me private one that's gone all to pot. I mean, with these two gals still not working a fortnight down the line, well, it's just not on, is it? To make matters worse, they've begun inviting some of their friends round to the flat, and I'm sure they're all on drugs cos there's times when I arrive home and the place is reeking of tobacco smoke. And it ain't the Golden Virginia type neither, that's for sure. What have I let myself in for? I asks meself despondently. Simon's debts seem to be never ending, with geezers popping up from all over the place demanding their dues, like. Slowly but surely I'm getting bled bleeding dry, ain't I? The latest is a three hundred quid beauty. A bloody car he's gone in for shortly before he's decided to call it a day, ain't it? I don't mind telling you, I'm getting pretty well browned off with it.

Then something happens this Saturday that makes me decide to pack me bags and get the hell out of it altogether – the lot – know what I mean? The flat, Simon's friends, the modelling game, every bloody thing. Get back to me old way of life, I'm thinking. You see, on this particular night in question after deciding on an early one and upon entering the flat, I finds various couples lying about all over the place smoking an' snoggin' an' everything. They're starkers, the bleeding lot of 'em, ain't they? And there's this bloody movie camera – what happens I've paid for – behind which some geezer is quite happily filming the sodding lot of 'em. I nearly has a fit, don't I? An' when I tries to put an end to their goings on, they nearly lynches me.

So, with no more ado I collects me bags and blows the coop, don't I? No, I don't want no part of this set up, I tell you, mate. I eventually inform the landlord of the situation, pays the rent owing, and leaves him to sort out the mess. I mean, I could end up the same way as Simon mixing with this bloody crowd, couldn't I? I gotta make the break and sort meself out, ain't I? After all, me main reason for coming to London in the first place was to hopefully become a pop singer, weren't it? Which is a joke now cos I ain't done no singing for ages, have I? No, sod it, I'm gonna throw it all in and get back to a civilised way of living with folk of me own kind, ain't I?

"Of course, it's your decision, Henry," me agent says when I tells him of me intentions. "I think you're making a mistake though, my son. Plenty of work around at the moment... and your face is getting well known on telly now. Could make yourself a lotta money if you put your mind to it, I know. Still, be that as it may, if you've decided to call it a day. I can also understand how upset you must be over Simon's loss, but never the less..."

Yeah, you'll never know, mate, I'm thinking to meself. But that's not the only reason why I want out, is it? You see, I've been suffering from a guilty conscience of late concerning my involvement in all of this business. I have this notion that I'm conning a lotta ordinary folk in what I'm doing. I mean, cigar an' toothpaste ads an' everything, crazy really ain't it? God! when I think of me ol' man and people like him having to slog away at their daily jobs for a mere pittance in comparison to what I've been earning for promoting dry bloody martini's an'all that crap, it don't bare thinking about, does it? And all the while half the bloody world is starving. Don't make sense, do it? But then, what does in this crazy old world we live in, eh? Not that I wanna bore you with all this philosophical jargon, like; but it does make you think, don't it?

"Even so," Ten Per Cent continues, puffing at a huge cigar, "you do have your own life to lead, Henry."

I looks at the geezer with disdain. "But that's just it, Ray," I says to him angrily. "I ain't at the moment, am I?"

So we parts company, don't we? On reasonably good terms, I might add, with no strings to hold me to a contract or anything like that, know what I mean?

"Well, good luck to you, son," Ray wishes me as we shakes hands. "If you feel like coming back anytime – give us a call, okay?"

So, with me guitar over me shoulder, I makes it down to Euston, don't I? Where I immediately gives me mum a ring before the train arrives.

"What's that? You're coming home – to stay?" she asks excitedly. "That's wonderful news, Henry… That will be nice. Never did like you up there in London, you know? Dad'll be pleased when I tell him."

"How's Carol – is she all right?" There's a long pause.

"Mum? Nothing's happened to her, has it?"

"She…she's in hospital. She's all right though."

An awful despairing feeling comes over me as I starts imagining all sorts of horrible things regarding Carol's well-being. "What you mean, in hospital? What's wrong with her for Chrissake?"

"I think you best come home as quick as you can, Henry…"

I slams the receiver down and hurries to catch me train without further ado. Chrissake! What the hell's going on? Carol in hospital? What on earth's happened to her? Life's certainly full of surprises lately, ain' it? What with poor ol' Simon – now Carol? Hope to God she's not had an accident or something? Enough to give you grey hairs, it is. The sooner I get home, the better, I'm thinking.

Chapter 14

I comes hurriedly out of Wufton Junction, not knowing whether to call in at the hospital first to see Carol, or pop home to me mum's to find out what's happening. The first person I encounters though is Rosy as I passes the cafeteria as she sits at the open window smoking a fag, her big boobs resting on the ledge and on display for all passers-by to see.

"An' where the hell are you dashin' off to in a great hurry then, 'Enry?" she enquires with a friendly smile. "An' where have you been hidin' yourself lately? Haven't seen you around these parts in ages. Thought perhaps you'd emigrated or somethin?"

"No, I'm still here, Rosy, luv," I informs her, stopping for a moment to admire the assets of this buxom blonde framed in the open window.

"Yeah, I seen you on the telly. Comin' up in the world, ain't we with you smokin' them great big fat cigars and drinkin' all those martinis? Bet yer get well paid for it, eh? Good luck to yer, mate – grab it while yer can, luv."

A fast train comes rushing through the station on its way to London, interrupting our intellectual conversation.

"What brings you back home then, 'Enry?" Rosy continues with our discussion when the sound of the train is no longer audible to our sensitive ears. "Here to see yer folks, are yer?"

"Yeah, you could say," I replies. "Wanna see Carol though. I hear she's in hospital?"

"Is she? It's the first I've heard of it. I don't see much of her these days though – so I wouldn't, would I? Wots a matter with her – nothin' serious, I hope?"

"Don't really know, Rosy. Only heard about it today meself from me mum, so I came straight down on the train. Anyway, I better hurry. I'll pop in and see you again soon now that I'm back in town. I'm giving up this modelling game, ain't I?"

Rosy throws her fag end out the window onto the pavement. "Get away – you must be mad – all that money you gotta be earning?"

"I'm serious, luv. Had enough, ain't I? It's not all its made out to be, I can tell you."

"I'm sorry to hear that, 'Enry. What will yer do with yerself now then? Not goin' back to Tarp's by any chance, are yer?"

Even I don't know that at the moment, I thinks to meself. I might, who knows? That's if the ol' sod'll have me back? I suppose leading the life I have lately has opened me eyes to a lotta things, that's for sure. I mean, you'll find no streakers or pot smokers at his workplace, I know? Just good old fashioned, healthy living workers. That's what I miss most, I think – the simple life.

"Not sure what I'll be doin'", I tells Rosy. "I'll keep in touch anyway."

"Course yer will, luv. Nothin' like 'avin' good friends to rely on, is there? Anyway, you get along to the 'ospital to see young Carol now. I do hope she's all right, 'Enry. Give her my love, won't yer?"

But I'm a fine one, ain't I? I don't know which hospital Carol's in, do I? So I drops in at Tarp's office on the way to acquire this information from him. After all, he's bound to know, ain't he?

"Carol's been admitted to the Pembrene Hospital, Higgins…Ward 3," the old fella informs me coldly. "I must say I didn't expect to see you this way again?"

"Why's that then?" I asks him contemptuously.

"Well, surely you must know the reason for Carol's hospitalisation, you…you scoundrel?"

I'm standing in front of the ol' geezer's desk just like I used to in the ol' days, ain't I? "No, should I then?" I questions him on the subject.

He sees that I'm pretty anxious for news of Carol, yet he persists in talking down to me, trying to make me feel small, like

I was still one of his employees or something, don't he? Know what I mean?

"Well! I must say," he gasps indignantly. "How impertinent? If you don't know the reason, Higgins, then you're an even bigger blackguard than I took you for."

I'm in complete ignorance as to what the hell he's rabbiting on about, ain't I? And I'm also getting pretty annoyed with him, I can tell you. I mean, what the hell is this all about anyway? Why can't he come straight to the point and just tell me what's ailing my Carol, for Chrissake! Instead of all this beating around the bleedin' bush?

"Well, I don't, do I?" I says to him angrily, raising me voice. "Perhaps you'll be good enough to tell me?"

The office door partly opens and ol' man Jenkins peers in at us. He looks the same as always, timid and frightened. "Is...is everything all right, Mr Tarp?" he enquires softly in his usual hesitant manner.

"Yes, yes...of course it is, Jenkins!" Tarp snaps at him. "Close the door and get back to your duties, man!"

The door closes quietly again, and I'm thinking to meself what a right bastard this Tarp geezer is. Christ! I wouldn't come back to work here no matter what, would I? Must have been bloody mad even contemplating the idea in the first place.

Then Tarp rises to his feet. "Yes, I'll tell you, shall I?" he begins calmly, before then exploding with rage: "For your information, Carol's having a baby! _Your_ baby, Higgins!"

I stands there, hardly able to take in what Tarp's just said. After all, what is the old sod implying? Then the penny drops, don't it? Of course – Pembrene is a maternity hospital, ain't it?

"_My_ baby!" I repeats finally, realising the true implication of this accusation aimed at me person, like.

"Yes, Higgins, that's right – _your_ baby – as if you didn't already know?"

It's all just too much, ain't it? What with Simon's tragic departure, I now have this piece of news to contend with, don't I? I mean, it's a right bleedin' shock to me system. Not on, is it?

"But...but when? " I asks in disbelief.

Then I gets this horrible feeling I'm being set up, don't I? You know what I mean?

"You sure it's my child she's having, and not yours?" I accuses Tarp of me suspicions.

At this suggestion, Tarp bangs his fist down hard onto the desk top.

"No, Higgins – it's not! Of this you can be quite sure. That's just the kind of immature remark I'd expect from you though. No doubt the same immature behaviour that led poor Carol astray in the first place? Irresponsible, that's what you are, Higgins. Always said so – always will. I wanted to marry the girl myself, you know? I still do despite her telling me she was expecting your child. Fancy running off and leaving her like you did – especially knowing her predicament?"

But now it's my turn to jump on me high horse, ain't it? "That's just it, you silly ol' sod – I didn't know, did I?" I shouts at him.

"Oh, don't play the innocent with me, Higgins. Of course you knew. You must have known."

I'm thinking that the whole of the office'll come running to Tarp's defence shortly if this here argument gets any more heated.

"She never told me – Carol never told me, I'm telling you. How was I supposed to know if no one even bothered telling me?"

It's time for the both of us to cool down, ain't it? Take stock of the situation.

"Well, now you do know, Higgins," Tarp utters, sitting himself down again to recover from his outburst at me. "Carol was admitted to hospital two days ago. They'll ring as soon as there's any news. Ward 3, as I've told you if you wish to visit her. Though heaven knows why she would ever want to see you again."

I grabs me guitar and hurriedly makes for the door. "Cos she loves me, that's why!" I says to him as a parting shot, leaving him sitting there sitting on his arse and brooding over this fact.

I bumps into Miss Pruce on the way out, don't I? "Hello! Henry," she greets me with a sweet smile.

"Hello! Miss Pruce," I replies politely, "how you keepin', luv?"

"I'm fine, thank you, Henry. I suppose you'll be off to see your young Carol, won't you?"

"Yeah, just about to. Didn't know, did I – about the baby?"

"She kept it a secret right up till this week, Henry. She'll be overjoyed to see you, I'm sure."

"She should have told me really. I feel terrible finding out like this."

"She must have had her reasons, Henry?"

I look deeply into the old dear's soft, blue eyes. "Tell me, Miss Pruce, is it true about Tarp wanting to marry Carol?"

Before answering, Miss Pruce looks over her shoulder to make sure no one's around, then answers: "It's common knowledge that he did, despite knowing about the baby; but your Carol refused him, didn't she? He took it badly. He's been like a bear with a sore head ever since. It's not very nice working here at the moment, Henry. I'm even thinking of leaving because of the bad atmosphere."

"Good for you, luv!"

"Yes, I've applied for a position with that soliciting firm across the road."

"Well, I'm sure it will be Tarp's loss and their gain if you get the job, Miss Pruce." I assures her. "Anyway, I best go see Carol, hadn't I?"

"Yes, you do that, Henry. Give her my love and tell her not to worry. I'm sure things will work out between you. Want to know something, young man? I think you are both well suited to each other."

I duly arrive at the hospital and finds me way along to the Ward in question.

"Miss Shelley's resting comfortably at the moment," the duty nurse informs me, looking me up and down as I stands there holding me guitar. Must have looked a right bloody nana, I know? Maybe I should serenade all the pregnant ladies in the ward while I'm here?

"Any chance of seeing her, please nurse?" I requests this pleasure.

"She's very tired. Perhaps you could come back this evening during visiting hours."

I won't be put off though, will I?

"But I've travelled all the way from London to see her. Won't do any harm – not had the baby yet, has she?"

The nurse, dressed in her starched, white uniform, stares at me for a moment, looking very sweet and very pretty.

"As a matter of fact she has," she breaks the news to me. "Miss Shelley had a fine baby boy less than fifteen minutes ago. Tell me-are you the Father, sir?"

That ol' sledge hammer deals me another mind shattering blow again, don't it? Now, it seems, I'm a bloody father!

I stands there just staring into space, me mouth agape, like.

"Seven pounds six ounces – lovely little chap!" Miss Starch enlightens me further.

A boy...! Bloody hell...! I – I can't believe it. Never even knew till today, did I? Yippee! I'm a bleedin' Father! "Where is she – where's my Carol?"

The nurse can see that I'm obviously overjoyed at the news. "Five minutes then, that's all," she grants me.

So I waltz down the Ward, gazing from bed to bed, trying to locate the mother of our baby. Other mothers, some holding their babies, some sleeping, occupy the other beds in the ward.

"You'll find Carol at the end on the right with the screen around her," the nurse kindly informs me.

I stops in front of the screen, not sure whether to go in around it to see Carol or not. Maybe she's still sleeping? And maybe she won't ever wanna see me again, like ol' Tarp says? I wanna see her though, don't I? Especially now. So I pluck up courage and goes in.

I stands looking down at her as she lays there resting on the bed, her fair hair partially covering one side of her face. She looks lovely, she really does. If you could see her you'd know what I mean. She's got this kinda special look, and she's wearing this pretty pink night- dress, ain't she? God! She is beautiful. Perhaps I should leave, not wake her? But there's such a lot I wanna say to her, ain't there? Especially now with the baby and everything. Our baby. Why did we ever split up? An' why the hell did I go and get mixed up with the crowd I did this past year? Complete bloody waste of time, wannit? No, my place is here with Carol and the baby, I know that now. I'll settle down, make a home for us all. Wave good-bye to the music and the modelling game. I'll get back with folk of me own kind in the real world. Know what I mean?

I reaches out to touch Carol's hand. Immediately, her beautiful blue eyes open to gaze up into mine.

"Henry!" she blinks in surprise at seeing me at her side and smiling a smile that even the bleedin' Mona Lisa couldn't manage, I'm sure. "It's nice to see you. How have you been keeping?"

By now I'm as weak as a kitten, ain't I? I've gone all soft inside and me legs are like jelly. Know what I mean? "I'm fine, thanks luv," I says, dropping to me knees to take her hands in mine and to nestle me head on her soft, warm, tummy.

"Oh, Henry," Carol sighs deeply. "I love you and I've missed you so much."

An' you wanna know something? I'm crying, ain't I? Just like a big baby. "And I love you too, Carol – more than anything, I know that now," I sobs uncontrollably.

"He really is a lovely baby, Henry. You did well. That fortune teller at Southend was right after all, wasn't she? She told us this would happen?"

Carol caresses the back of me neck with her soft hand.

"Why didn't you tell me about the baby, Carol? Don't you think I had the right to know? After all, I am the Father."

Carol remains silent for a few moments. "I…I didn't want you to think I might trap you in this way, that's why, Henry," she tells me finally.

I lifts me head to gaze into her blue eyes. "You're too good for me, you know that, don't you? Much too good."

She holds my gaze with an innocent look on her face. "I wouldn't want to force you into anything, Henry. I'd sooner you went away now than stay on – maybe to regret it later?" she says to me sweetly.

"Don't talk silly, luv. I want you now more than ever. And the kid. By the way – what shall we call him?"

Carol squeezes me hand. "We'll name him after you, of course. He'll be our little Henry, won't he? Oh, Henry…I…I'm so happy."

That's settled then, ain't it? An' me an' Carol eventually gets married at the local registry office, don't we? Henry junior is also in attendance so as we can obtain a birth certificate for him at the same time. We are blessed with a nice sunny day for the occasion, and after the ceremony we hold the reception down at the Labour Club where both our folks, friends and relatives are gathered to celebrate our happy event. Jason and Stench are there along with the mayor and his wife. The landlord from the local, Tom Bassett and his good lady is also present. So we're all one big happy family really, ain't we? After the scoff and usual speeches is over, our singing cowboy friend, Randy Bates provides us all with some entertainment, like. We also have a small Band along so as to encourage all the aspiring Fred Astaire's and Ginger Rogers's present onto the floor for some waltzes and foxtrots. Would have been nice to have invited our Mr Sinatra along to sing us all a few songs, but I don't think even some of us, despite our reputation, could manage to pull that off somehow, do you? By the way – me best man at the wedding is me old school mate, Spud Milligan, remember him? Yeah, he comes down with his latest piece of skirt to do the honours, don't he? Does me proud as well, not putting a foot or a word wrong all day, I'm happy to say. Some of the other guests includes dear ol' Miss Pruce and Mr Jenkins. Tarp himself even gets an invite from us, don't he? He chooses not to attend though – which is just as well really, cos the temptation to punch him one straight on the nose might have proved too great for me, mightn't it? I don't think he's got over the fact of losing Carol to me, has he? Still, as I say, all's fair in love an' war, ain't it? So we makes do without him as Randy goes into action after the last toast of the evening is offered up.

"Yippee – yi – yeh…! – Yippee – yi – yo…!"

"Least you got show business out of your system, lad?" the mayor says to me afterwards, smoking his big cigar, referring, of course, to me past years' experience, like.

"Swell party ya havin', Henree, ma…rn," Jason drawls, almost under the table now by the amount of scotch he's consumed in the past hour.

"Nice seein' you look so smart, me ol' son," me dad compliments Stench on his neat appearance for this momentous occasion.

"Looks okay when I turns me mind to it," Stench proudly answers, gulping his beer, being extra careful not to spill any on his fine suit of clothes.

"I'm glad you and Carol's finally decided to get back together in this way, Henry," me mum sighs happily, sipping her glass of stout. "Never did like you working up there in London."

"Do not forsake me, oh, my darlin'…!" Randy leads into another song, cracking his whip high above his fancy piece who's sitting down in front of him smoking and drinking whilst listening to her hero perform.

"Ooo! You just wait till I get you home this evening, Randy!" she swoons up at him with excitement.

"Owner of an 'orse now, 'Enry," Tom Bassett informs me with a smile, sporting a gigantic pink carnation in the lapel of his pinstriped suit.

"What the hell you gonna do with an 'orse, for Chrissake?" I asks, sitting back, feeling a very proud young man with me blushing bride seated next to me at my side.

"To ride – what you think? Great pastime. Can't beat an early morning canter up on that field behind the rubbish tip before opening the pub."

"By the way, Tom, is Basher still working for you?"

"No, we parted company ages ago. Had to let him go. The Disco evenings all came to an end, didn't they? Bloody kids spoiled it for themselves. Drugs, you know? Police got involved – couldn't have that, could I? Bad for business. Not losing my bloody licence over them, that's for sure."

"Yeah, I know what you mean," I reflects, thinking of how poor old Simon ended up.

"I believe Basher's body guarding for the pop stars these days. Still makin' a fortune, I hear. Anyway, you'd never recognise the old pub now, Henry? Completely re-modernised from top to bottom. By the way, any thoughts about what kinda work you'll be looking for now that you're back in town?"

"No, not really. Stay with me folks, I suppose, till I gets meself sorted. Put me name on the housing list for a start. Reckon that'll be a long wait. Gotta be done though."

Tom sips his ale. "I could fix you up with a job, Henry, tide you over till something else comes along?"

"Doing what?" I enquires with interest.

"Potman! Ours left last week."

Would you believe it, eh? A bloody potman! After all I done to get to the bleedin' top… and I'm offered a position of this magnitude. Unbelievable. Funny ol' world we live in, ain't it?

"Dunno. Might be interested," I says to his offer, not too proud to turn it down, considering the ways things is for me at present, like.

"Give it some thought, Henry?"

"Yeah, I will."

Our reception finally comes to an end, don't it? During the course of the evening, I'm given little titbits of information from various friends as to what's been happening in Wufton during me absence, like. I learns that me an' Carol's folks has recently come up trumps at Bingo, ain't they? Each of 'em winning five hundred quid! Better than a smack in the eye any day, I know? I suppose if you was to reckon it out though over the years they've spent trying for a prize, then it might just about cover what they've laid out to get it in the first place, don't it? Other items of interest is that a Darby an' Joan Club building has recently been built and stands on the green alongside the Catholic church where we used to play football when we was kids and is going to be officially opened by the mayor this coming Saturday. All very well catering for the ol' folk, but where on earth are the kids going to kick ball in the future now then is what I'm wondering. This pastime certainly kept us youngsters out of mischief and away from the strong arm of the law, that's for sure. I wonder what the hell the present-day ones will get up to now. Makes you think, dunnit? Oh, an' the council has also decided to demolish a number of old prefab's up on the estate to make way for some new houses to be built in their place. 'Bout time, too, if you ask me. Crikey! They was erected shortly after the Second World War, weren't they? So I reckon it's time they went, don't you? When you think about it though, it's certainly a problem housing everyone in the world, ain't it? I suppose there will always be a shortage of accommodation really with people without roofs over their heads, won't there? Terrible thought, ain't it? Can't ever see a solution to this problem neither, can you? But enough of politics for now, eh? Mustn't let it spoil me an' Carol's wedding celebrations, must we? But it does seriously make you think, dunnit?

As the evening draws to its close, me old man takes me to one side for a word in private, don't he? At first, I think he's going to give me a lecture on the birds and the bees, like, seeing as it's me wedding night, and to maybe give me a few pointers on the right way to go about doing what all new honeymooners does on this particular night, don't I? But he doesn't. No, he just wants to thank me for helping make come true his dream of seeing his favourite entertainer live in person, don't he?

"You'll never know how much that meant to me, Son," he says to me very humbly. "And without you, I don't think it would have ever been possible. From the bottom of my heart, I thank you, Henry."

At this point, we both embrace, which is a good thing for any father and son to do at any time, ain't it? But especially at this particular moment in one's life after having just got married.

"S'all right, Pa," I answers him with deep affection between hugs. "I'm really glad we managed to pull it off together. It most certainly will be something to tell your grandson later on in life now, won't it?"

Breaking free from each other's arms and with a broad, happy grin spread all over his face, me old man jokes: "It sure as hell will, Henree! It sure as hell will!"

Even Jason couldn't have summed it up better now, could he?

Anyway, it's now time for the last waltz of the evening, ain't it? So I grabs me blushing bride, and we takes to the floor to lead the way for others to do likewise. I notices me folks teaming up together, also Carol's , which is nice to see, to no doubt show all us youngsters present how to really go about performing the art of ballroom dancing.

"Are you happy, Henry?" me lovely wife enquires as I try to match her excellent dance steps to the best of me ability on our way 'round the floor. You see, I'm not all that good a dancer, am I? I does me best though, don't I?

"Yes, very," I answers Carol truthfully. "Happier than I've ever been in me life, luv."

"I'm so glad to hear that, my darlin'."

We're both holding each other very close, and I don't want this dance to ever end, do I? I now know how Cinderella must have felt at the midnight hour with her coach waiting to take her home to spoil the one magical evening in her life, don't I? Nothing of this nature is going to ruin our evening, is it? Even though a chauffeur-driven limousine that the mayor's laid on that day for the wedding is waiting outside the Club to whisk us away once the celebrations is all complete, like. Nice of the ol' boy to loan us the use of this, don't you think? After all, I believe he's only allowed to use it on special, civic occasions himself during the year, ain't he?

"I love you, Henry, and I will try to make you happy, I promise."

"And I love you too, Carol," I confesses as I gaze into her gorgeous eyes. "And I promise that I shall do my best for you and little Henry, come what may."

"Oh, Henry, I know you will," she says, smiling happily as we continues to dance with carefree abandonment.

So, after all the guests is finally gone and we're back at my folks' place in my old room, I'm as happy as a sandboy lying in bed with me newly-wed by me side and with Henry junior in his cot next to us, ain't I? In fact, I don't ever remember feeling so happy in me life before, despite not knowing what exactly the future has in store for us at this stage in our lives. Whatever will be, will be, I suppose?

"Who'd of thought, Henry," my beautiful bride lying beside me whispers in the still, quietness of our room, "that Mr Tarp would send a telegram wishing us every happiness in the world?"

"Yeah, I never expected he would, I gotta admit," I confesses to her.

"Nice of him though, wasn't it?"

"Yeah, really nice. Just goes to show that miracles do happen sometimes, don't they? I can't help feeling sorry for the ol' sod though. After all, he was only looking for some happiness – same as all of us really, weren't he?"

I holds me little darlin' close in my arms. "Wanna know something, luv?"

"What's that, Henry?"

"I know I've found mine."

She caresses me lovingly and purrs assuredly in my ear: "Oh, so have I, Henry, so have I."

The End